The Solar Advocate

By

Larry Waitz

Copyright 2009

LDW Publishing
Oceanside, NY

The Solar Advocate

2010, I am entering my fifth year, of my second chapter, of moral duty to solarizeing America. The first chapter started in 1975, while attending Ohio University in Athens, Ohio. As the energy prices were getting higher, alternative energy was becoming increasingly more popular. It was an exciting time for solar energy in America, with Solar DHW (domestic hot water) leading the way. It was the early 80s when the solar trend started to reverse itself with cheap energy prices, and a political administration that just laughed at solar energy.

It was 2005 when I was visiting family in New York, when I was reading an article in the local newspaper, that LIPA (Long Island Power Authority), the local utility was offering a rebate approximately 45% of the cost, for any of their customers, using PV's (Photovoltaic's) to generate electricity from the sun. It was that article that brought me back into the solar energy market! With the Federal government, most State governments, and more and more Utilities standing behind this new increased solar movement, by offering incentives, whether they are in the form of tax credits, and or actual rebates. In 2010 PV's are leading this new Solar charge, with Solar thermal (heating water) following. On the thermal side of solar, domestic hot water systems are now being delivered in pre-engineered packages, and more aesthetically pleasing. I am very pleased to report that generating electricity from the sun, and generating heated water for domestic hot water, with the products available today, works so well, that Solar energy should be taken off the "Alternative" energy list and made a Choice!

The Solar Advocate is an introduction to solar energy for anybody interested in knowing where we stand in the US, with respect to solar applications, usage, and the practicality. The time is now, that all home/building owners should know all of their choices when selecting an energy source for the home or small business. The time for solar energy has never been better!

The Solar Advocate will give the reader arguments **for** the use of solar energy in the United States. The book has 66 characteristics of solar energy which are the talking points of the book. I follow these characteristics with over 300 general facts on solar energy, conventional fossil fuel, renewable energy, and anything that will assist my argument **for** the logic of solar energy in our everyday lives.

The Solar Advocate will assist you in your new solar energy journey. Whether you will be generating electricity from the sun, or heating hot water, the products are available today for you (US) to make a difference. Enjoy the journey!

Larry Waitz
Larrywaitz@Thesolaradvocate.com

The Solar Advocate

Table of Contents

66 Characteristics of Solar Energy

1	Renewable	1

Renewable energy sources are maintained or replaced by nature. Wind, hydropower, geothermal, biofuels, and biomass are additional renewable energy choices.

Did You Know :
   The Sun is a star, one of billions and billions, and billions…

Really!
   The diameter of our galaxy, the Milky Way, is 100,000 light years across.
   5,878,499,810,000,000,000 miles,
   with the average thickness being 1000 light years, or
   5,878,499,810,000,000 miles

Energy Facts:
   For each gallon of gas that an automobile burns, it will create 20 pounds of CO_2.

Wow
The Sun is between 26,000, and 30,000 light years from the center of our Milky Way galaxy, and it takes 250,000,000 years for Earth to orbit its own galaxy.

The Universe

The age of the Universe is said to be 14 billion years old.
The Universe contains 200-300 galaxies.
In our galaxy, the Milky Way, there are between 200 and 400 billion stars!
Our Universe contains anywhere from 40,000-120,000 billion Suns.

Earth is traveling at 140 mi/s around the Milky Way, and the Milky Way is traveling at 190 mi/s, making Earth traveling a total of 330 mi/s! At that speed we can make it from New York to California and back in less than 30 seconds.

Astronomical unit (AU) is the average distance from Earth to the Sun = 92,955,807 miles.

Our Solar System

Planet	Diameter (miles)	Distance from Sun (AU)	Length of day (Earthday)	Length of year (days)	Solar insolation (W/m^2)	Weight 150 lb Earthling	Age 50 yr Earthling
Mercury	3031	0.387	58	88	9116	57	21
Venus	7519	0.723	243	225	2611	136	81.27
Earth	7924	1	1	365	1366	150	50
Mars	4216	1.5	1	6860	588	56	26.59
Jupiter	88,709	5.2	0.41	12 Y	50.5	354	4.22
Saturn	74,955	9.53	0.44	29 Y	15.04	137	1.7
Uranus	31,755	19	0.72	84 Y	3.72	133	0.6
Neptune	30,767	30	0.67	164 Y	1.5	168	0.29
Pluto	1428	39.5	6	247 Y	0.087	8	0.2

Solar System Composition
% of Mass
Sun   99.85%
Planets 0.135%
Comets 0.01%
Satellites 0.00005%
Minor Planets may be 0.0000002%
Meteorites – minimal

The Solar Advocate

99.85% of all matter in our Solar system is contained in the Sun, and since energy is related to mass, I am sleeping well at night knowing that the Sun will be able to provide Earth with energy without ever running out, in my lifetime.

Did You Know
That our climate and weather are driven by the Sun's energy, and the Sun supports **all life** on Earth?

Really!
All planets travel clockwise and very close to the same plane, just like the galaxy.

Really!
An Earthling weighing 150 pounds will weigh 2400 pounds on the Sun.

Wow!
You can fit over 1 million Earths into the Sun.

The Sun and the Earth

The Sun is a giant natural fusion thermal nuclear reactor converting hydrogen to helium, and releases
3.3×10^{27} kWh/yr

33,000,000,000,000,000,000,000,000,000 kWh/yr

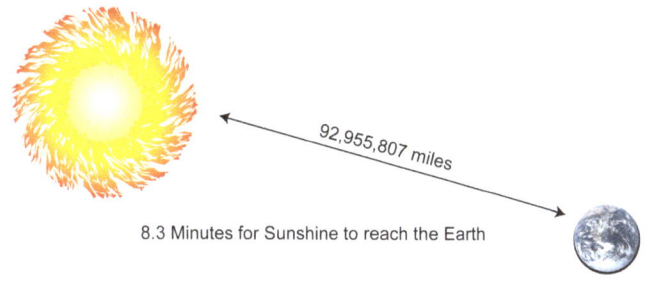

92,955,807 miles

8.3 Minutes for Sunshine to reach the Earth

Sun – Earth Comparison

	Sun	Earth
Diameter (miles)	864,988	7920
Mass (pounds)	4.37×10^{30}	13.2×10^{24}
Volume (cubic feet)	3.58×10^{17}	2.5×10^{11}
Average density (kg/m^3)	1400	5506
Surface gravity	274	9.81
Rotational Period (days)	28	1
Temperature at the surface (°F)	10,000	68

The Sun is 4 billion years old, with 5 billion years to go.

The Sun loses mass at a rate of 700 million tons/second.

Solar winds blow at 280 mi/s.

It takes **8.3 minutes** for Solar radiation to reach the Earth at the speed of light, which is 186,000 mi/s.

1 **light year** equals traveling the speed of light (186,000 mi/s) for one year.
(186,000 mi/s x 365 days/yr x 24 hours/day x 60 minutes/hour x 60 s/min)
5,878,499,810,000 miles
or
63,241,077 AU.

3	Reliable	3

You can rely on the Sun coming up every morning and setting every night. After the 20,000 nights I have gone to sleep, I can safely say that the Sun will be there in the morning, and will set some time in the evening.

 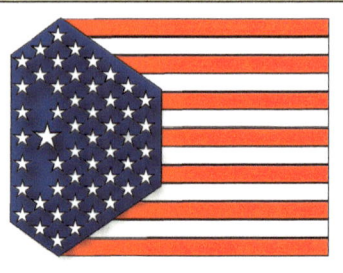 

Did You Know
That Solar energy is extremely practical and is slowly coming off the alternative energy list and is now becoming a choice?

Really!
Egyptian Sun God – Ra
Aztec Sun God – Huitzilopochtli & Tezcatlipoca
Japanese Sun God – Amaterasu

Energy Facts
United States land receives 9 x 10^{15} kWh/yr
9,000,000,000,000,000 kWh/yr
from the Sun.

Wow!
If an Egyptian were to call to its Sun God Ra, it would take 13.8 years for Ra to receive the worshiper's prayer (at the speed of sound which is 768 mph) and the worshiper would have to wait 27.6 years at a minimum for an answer!

The Solar Advocate

The Solar Constant

The Solar constant is the amount of Solar radiation that hits the Earth's atmosphere.

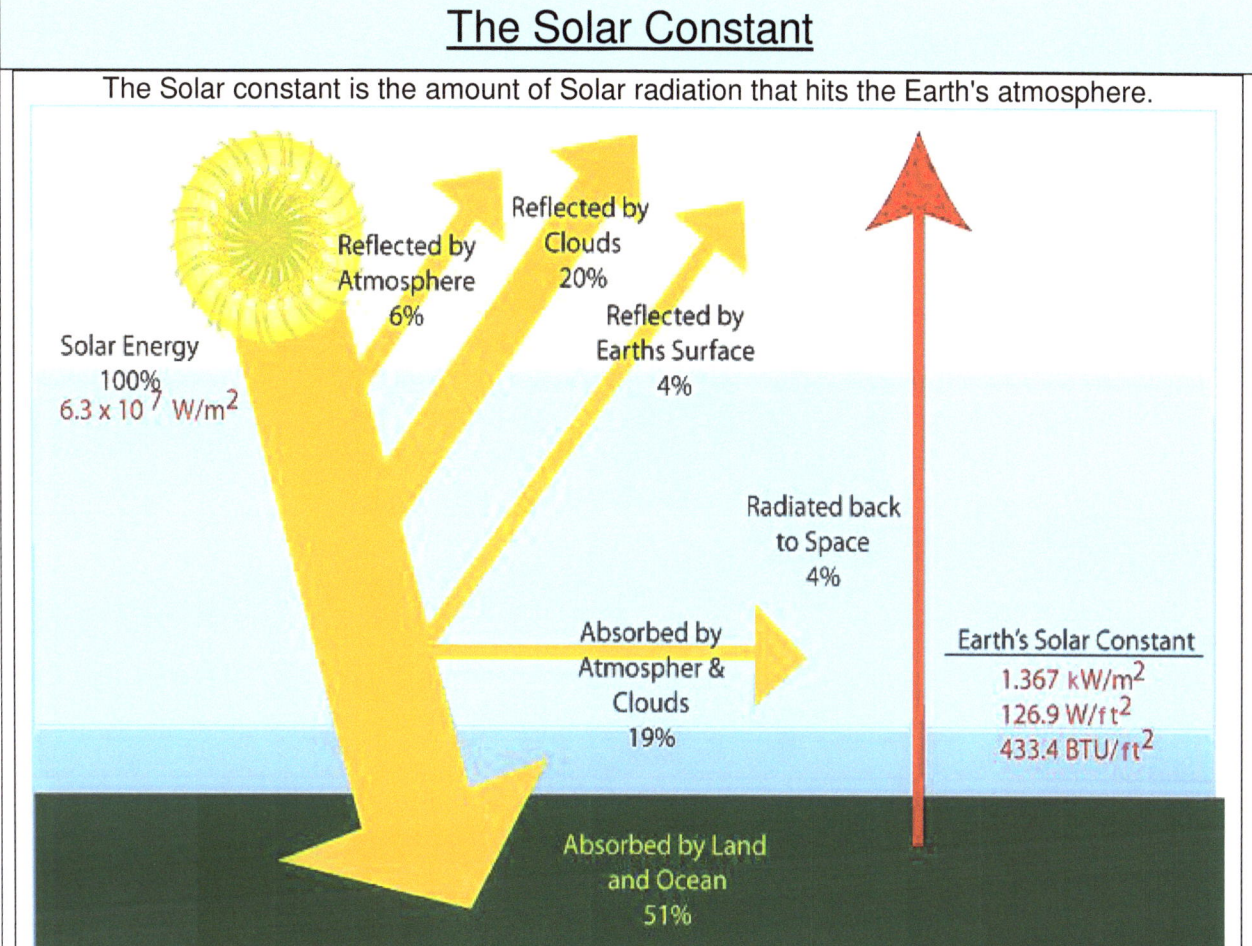

Solar Energy Effects	**The Sun's Rays Are Reflected by:**
Sunlight	Pollution
Rain	Dust
Snow	Clouds
Wind	Air
Hail	Water vapor
Fog	Forest fires
Air density	Erupted volcanoes
Temperature	Smog

4	Predictable	4

The Sun rises in the east and sets in the west. In the northern hemisphere, the Sun will always be on the southern horizon. Modern technology can give us the sunrise and sunset times of anywhere in the world at any given time. If you are interested in these values for your location, I invite you to the website http://aa.usnonavmil/data/docs/RS_OneDay.php

 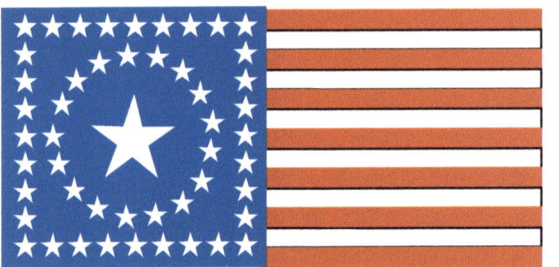 

Did You Know

That gravity holds the Sun intact?

Really!

The amount of Solar radiation hitting Lake Mead is five times the amount of power that the Hoover Dam puts out in a year.

Energy Facts

The United States represents 5% of the world population,
yet we consume 21% of the world's energy.
The world consumes 462 quads of energy
and the United States consumes 101 quads of energy.

Do the Math

The speed of light is 186,000 mi/s, and at that speed you can travel 7-1/2 times around the Earth in a second.

  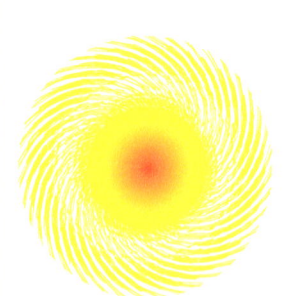

Electromagnetic Spectrum

Solar radiation can be broken down into
41% visible
9% UV
50% infrared

The electromagnetic spectrum below shows us the Solar radiation that is received on Earth.

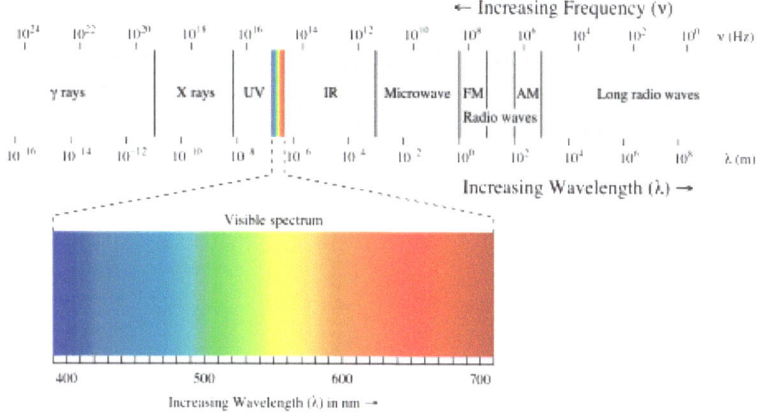

Ultraviolet C
Because of its size, most of it is absorbed in the atmosphere.

Ultraviolet B
Is responsible for the photochemical reaction which produces the ozone layer.

Ultraviolet A
A popular use is tanning, and is not damaging to DNA.

Visible Range
Visible light is what we see with our naked eye.

Infrared
Is responsible for the heat and warmth on Earth
Infrared A – 700 nm-1400 nm
Infrared B – 1400 nm-3000 nm
Infrared C – 3000 nm-1 mm

5	Pollution Free	5

Natural gas, oil, electric, propane, and wood heating systems all have chimneys. Solar PV and Solar Thermal Systems do not require chimneys! No chimneys, no pollution!

Did You Know
Since 1856, when we started keeping records on global temperatures, 1995 was the warmest on record?

Really!
King Solomon ordered his soldiers to use their highly polished shields with the Sun to blind the Egyptian army.

Energy Facts
Power companies produce 3.3 to 4.2 kWh for each 1 kilowatt delivered.

Wow!
Utilizing only 1% of the world's deserts, Solar Energy can replace fossil fuel usage!

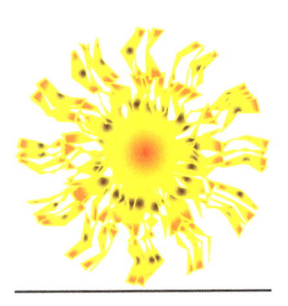
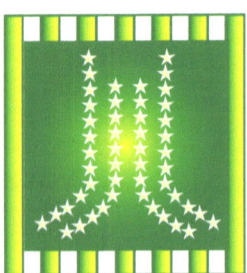

Solar Applications

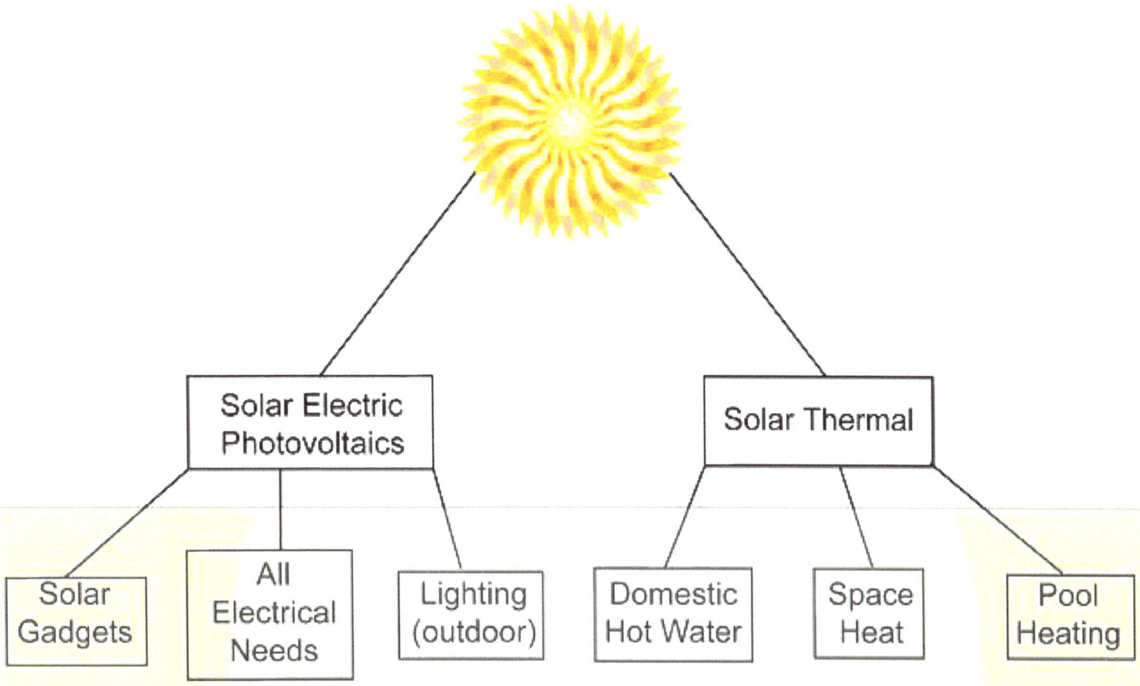

Solar Electric Photovoltaics

Solar Thermal

Solar Gadgets

All Electrical Needs

Lighting (outdoor)

Domestic Hot Water

Space Heat

Pool Heating

To be discussed in book:

Residential, Commercial, and Agricultural will all be covered!
The basic difference between these items are the size of the system.
The same basic principles hold true for both PV and Thermal.

Each State or Local Utility will have their own Rebate or Tax Incentive structure.
Check with your Installer for details.

What this book will not cover:

Solar Cooking
Industrial Process Heat
Concentrating Collectors
Expermental modules, and collectors
Solar Vehicles
Solar Air-Conditioning

The Solar Advocate

Have you ever heard the Sun? Absolutely not! The Sun is responsible for thunder, lightning, and wind, with some of the loudest sounds I've ever heard. The Sun makes it through the atmosphere with no sound at all. On a Solar DHW system, the only sound comes from a very small pump, which you would have to stand right up to in order to hear it. On the Solar PV side, the only moving part is a small fan in the inverter box, and this is generally outside. Noise pollution will never be a situation with Solar.

Did You Know

In 2007, America consumed approximately 20,687,000 barrels of oil per day?

Really!

The summer Sun is farther than the winter Sun by 3,000,000 miles. On January 3, when the Sun is closest to the Earth, the United States is in its cold season.

Energy Facts

The average U.S. car that gets 20 miles to the gallon will emit 50 tons of CO_2 over the lifetime of the car.

Did You Know

Solar energy is the most available energy source Earth knows?

The Solar Advocate

Sun and Moon Schedule

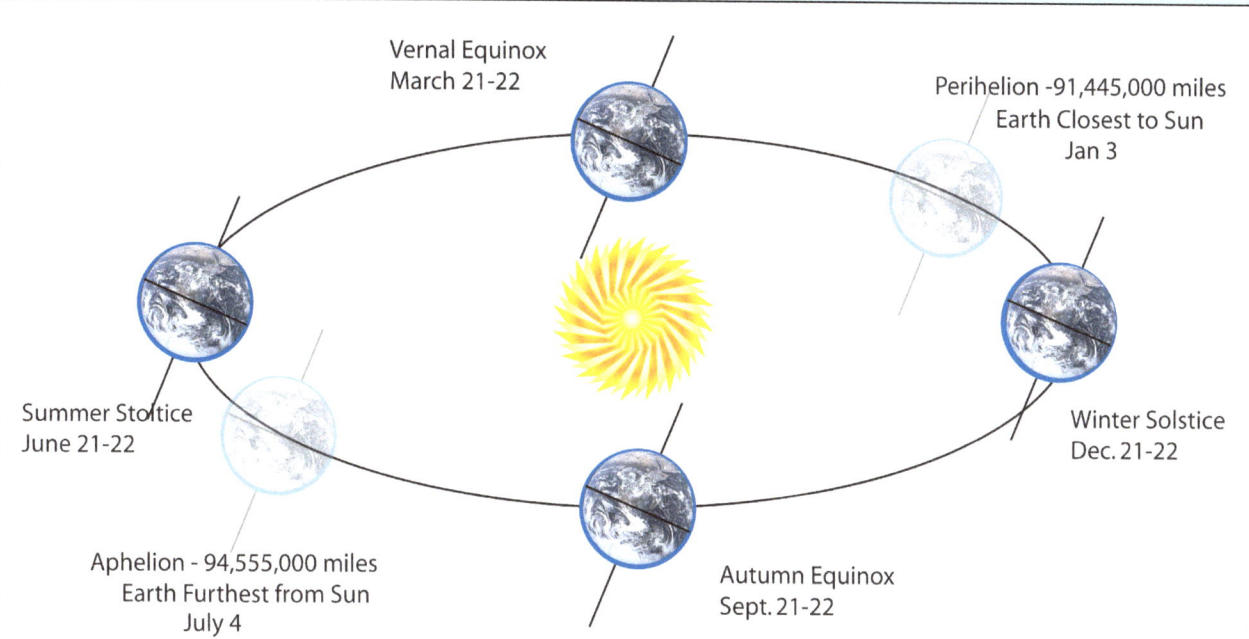

Vernal Equinox
March 21-22

Perihelion -91,445,000 miles
Earth Closest to Sun
Jan 3

Summer Stoltice
June 21-22

Winter Solstice
Dec. 21-22

Aphelion - 94,555,000 miles
Earth Furthest from Sun
July 4

Autumn Equinox
Sept. 21-22

Sunrise and Sunsets

Add one hour for daylight savings time if and when in use.

City	State	Latitude	Longitude	Zip	December 21	Fall/Spring 21	June 21
NYC	New York	41	74	10001	7:16/4:32	5:42/5:54	4:25/7:30
LA	California	34	118	90001	6:55/4:48	5:41/5:51	4:43/7:08
Chicago	Illinois	41	87	60601	7:15/4:23	5:37/7:49	4:16/7:29
Houston	Texas	29	95	77053	7:13/5:27	6:10/6:19	5:22/7:25
Philadelphia	Pennsylvania	39	75	19113	7:19/4:39	5:47/5:59	4:32/7:33
Phoenix	Arizona	33	112	85001	7:29/5:25	6:16/6:26	5:19/7:42
San Diego	California	33	117	92101	6:47/4:47	5:36/5:46	4:41/7:00
Dallas	Texas	33	97	75252	7:26/5:25	4:15/6:25	5:20/7:38
San Jose	California	37	122	95101	7:82/4:54	5:55/6:05	4:47/7:31
Detroit	Michigan	42	83	48201	7:58/5:03	6:19/6:31	4:56/8:13
Indianapolis	Indiana	39	86	46280	8:02/5:23	6:31/6:43	5:17/8:16
Columbus	Ohio	39	85	43240	7:50/5:10	6:19/6:30	5:03/8:04
Baltimore	Maryland	38	76	21240	7:23/4:47	5:53/6:05	4:40/7:27
Memphis	Tennessee	36	86	37501	7:04/4:52	5:47/5:58	4:46/7:18
Seattle	Washington	47	122	98101	7:55/4:20	5:55/6:08	4:11/8:11
Portland	Oregon	45	122	97222	7:48/4:30	5:57/6:09	4:22/8:03
Boston	Massachusetts	42	71	02108	7:10/4:15	5:31/5:43	4:08/7:25
Denver	Colorado	39	104	80221	7:18/4:39	5:47/5:58	4:32/7:31

7	Minimal Maintenance	7

The maintenance factor for Solar is minimal. It is advised to have service calls yearly, but not necessarily in most cases. Once installed, keep an eye on the collectors or modules for any excess dirt, and wash off accordingly. In most cases a hose will do the trick. On the PV side, check your monitor, it tells all. On the thermal side, keep an eye on the pH of your Solar fluid every 3 to 5 years. Outside of these items, not much else has to be done.

  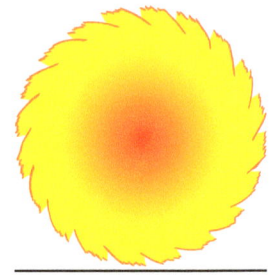

Did You Know
Only 7.5% of our energy consumption came from renewable sources in the United States in 1999? 94% of that total was in the form of hydropower (dams) and biomass (wood).

Really!
It was 1885 when Scientific American published a story on using flat plate collectors to be placed on roofs for commercial applications.

Energy Facts
In 2008, the United States installed 830 MW of photovoltaics
In 2008, Germany installed 3,862 MW (3.862 GW) of photovoltaics!

Do the Math
In New York state, the Robert Moses Niagara Plant (Niagara Falls) is one of the largest hydroelectric plants (renewable) in the world, with an output of 2.253 GW.

 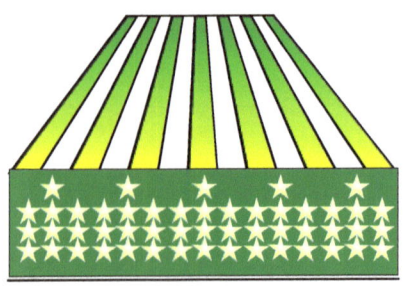 

Sunshine Intensity

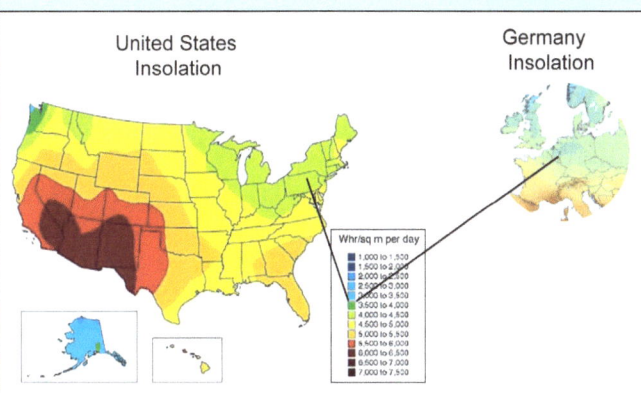

United States
Insolation

Germany
Insolation

Whr/sq m per day

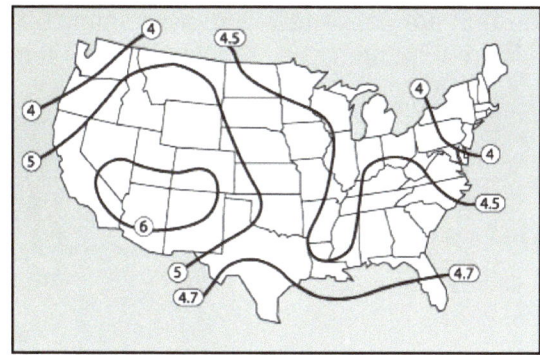

Is there enough Sunshine hitting the United States for Solar Energy to work?

The above map shows the **Insolation** (W/m^2) of the United States and Germany. Germany's best Solar insolation does not equal our worst insolation conditions, which is in the northeastern United States. The Solar conditions only get better as you go west and south. Does Solar energy work in America? The Solar products being discussed in this book will all work in the vast majority of America. The map on the right will show you the average amount of sunshine hours for the country.

Insolation Values (W/m^2)

City	State	Insolation – Fixed-Latitude (W/m^2)	Insolation Tracking E-W Latitude (w/m^2)*	Insolation 2-Way Tracking (W/m^2)**
NYC	New York	4.6	5.6	5.8
LA	California	5.6	7.0	7.2
Chicago	Illinois	4.4	5.5	5.7
Houston	Texas	4.8	6.0	6.2
Philadelphia	Pennsylvania	4.6	5.7	5.9
Phoenix	Arizona	6.5	8.6	8.9
San Diego	California	5.7	7.2	7.4
Dallas	Texas	5.4	6.9	7.2
San Jose	California	5.4	6.9	7.1
Detroit	Michigan	4.2	5.3	5.5
Indianapolis	Indiana	4.6	5.7	5.9
Columbus	Ohio	4.2	5.3	5.4
Baltimore	Maryland	4.6	5.9	6.0
Memphis	Tennessee	5.0	6.4	6.6
Seattle	Washington	3.7	4.7	4.9
Portland	Oregon	3.9	4.9	5.1
Boston	Massachusetts	4.6	5.7	5.9
Denver	Colorado	5.5	7.2	7.4

* Tracking the Sun from east to west
** Tracking the Sun from east to west, and north to south

8	## Will Never Run Out of Fuel	8

The Sun's power is estimated at 386 billion billion megawatts. Every second 700,000,000 tons of hydrogen are converted to approximately 695,000,000 tons of helium with 5000 tons of energy, in the form of gamma rays, emitted. With that much power, will we ever run out of Solar fuel?

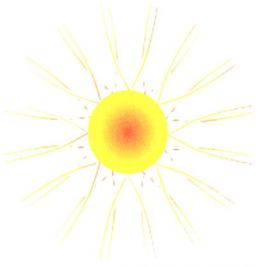

Did You Know
That the Sun's radiation can supply electricity as well as heat? The applications of Solar energy today generally fall within these two categories: electric and thermal.

Really!
The temperature in the Sun's core is 50,000,000 °C.

Energy Facts
The average nuclear power plant generated 12.5 billion kWh per year.
That's 65 plants with 104 operating reactors, for a total of
808.97 billion kWh/year.

Do the Math
12.5 billion kilowatt hours per year =
102,739,726 kWh per month =
3,424,657 kWh per day
@1000 kilowatt hours per month – average household usage.
A 12 .5 billion kWh nuclear reactor will service approximately 102,739 households.

Conventional Energy

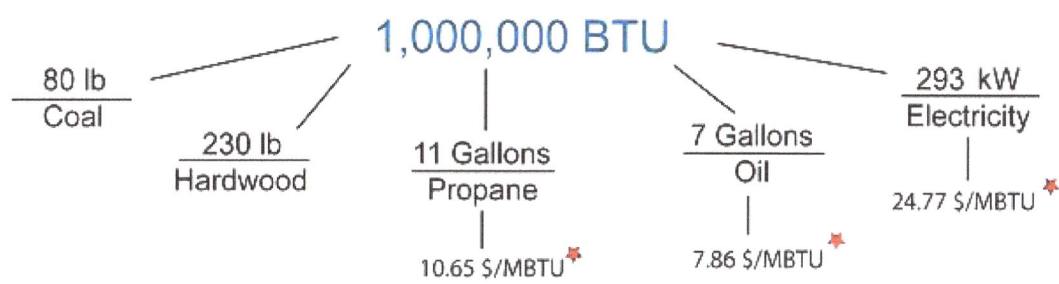

1,000,000 BTU

- 80 lb Coal
- 230 lb Hardwood
- 11 Gallons Propane — 10.65 $/MBTU *
- 7 Gallons Oil — 7.86 $/MBTU *
- 293 kW Electricity — 24.77 $/MBTU *

Fuel	Unit Measure	Energy Content (BTU)	Pounds of CO_2 per unit
Natural gas	cubic feet	1030	12.1
Propane	gallons	91,000	12.7
Gasoline	gallons	125,000	19.6
Oil	gallons	140,000	22.4
Firewood	cord	25,000	3,814
Coal	pounds	13,000	4,166
Nuclear (breeder)	Pounds	20,000,000,000	NA
Nuclear(no breeder)	Pounds	500,000,000	NA
Solar	Square feet	1500 per day	0

Fuel	Total # households	%	2008 Price
Natural gas	56,286,013	50	$1.33/therm
LP	6,420,250	5.7	$2.50 per gallon
Electric	36,739,794	33	$0.14 per kWh
Fuel oil	8,599,960	7.7	$3.40 per gallon
Coal	113,807	0.1	NA
Wood	1,976,841	1.7	NA
Solar	32,142	0.02	Varies
Other or none	1,416,826	1.2	Varies

What goes into Pricing Energy

	Oil	Natural Gas	Coal	Nuclear	Solar
Raw materials – cost	Y	Y	Y	Y	NO
Conversion – cost	Y	Y	Y	Y	NO
Transportation – cost	Y	Y	Y	Y	NO
Energy Content	High	Med	Med	High	LOW
Maintenance	Y	Y	Y	Y	Minimal

★ These are average prices from across the country, and can change suddenly, or not at all. Keep an eye on your bill for the latest prices on fuel.

9	**Will Decrease Oil Imports**	9

The practicality of Solar DHW (domestic hot water) today can easily decrease the amount of oil we import from overseas. As more and more people go the Solar route, I am sure that the goal of reduced oil imports will be achieved. Oil independence in 10 years?

Did You Know

That 25% of the average American home energy bill goes to domestic hot water (DHW)? Solar DHW is looking at the best potential to save 70 to 80% of your DHW costs within a five-year payback.

Really!

The average home contributes more air pollution than the average car!

Energy Facts

Nine Year Price Schedule-Natural Gas $/tcf (trillion cubic feet)								
2000	2001	2002	2003	2004	2005	2006	2007	2008
$3.95	$4.43	$3.35	$5.17	$5.81	$8.12	$6.88	$6.87	$8.69
120% increase over nine years For Natural Gas								
Nine year Price schedule-barrels of oil (42 gallons)								
2000	2001	2002	2003	2004	2005	2006	2007	2008
$22.68	$21.77	$17.06	$28.52	$27.67	$33.79	$53.26	$51.57	$88.41
Almost 300% increase over nine years for a barrel of oil.								

Really!

The Suns behavior cycle is every 11 years.

Sun Path Charts

Sun Path Charts is a plot of the Sun's elevation angle, and azimuth angle. In designing Solar energy systems, a Sun chart would be useful in shading analysis, whether it be for passive building design or Solar obstruction analysis. The place to go for an accurate, printed Sun chart for your location is: http://Solardat.uoregon.edu/SunChartProgram.html, where all you need is a zip code. The results will show where the Sun will be at any given time of the day, month, or year. It is a very good tool to understand how the Sun travels throughout the year for your location.

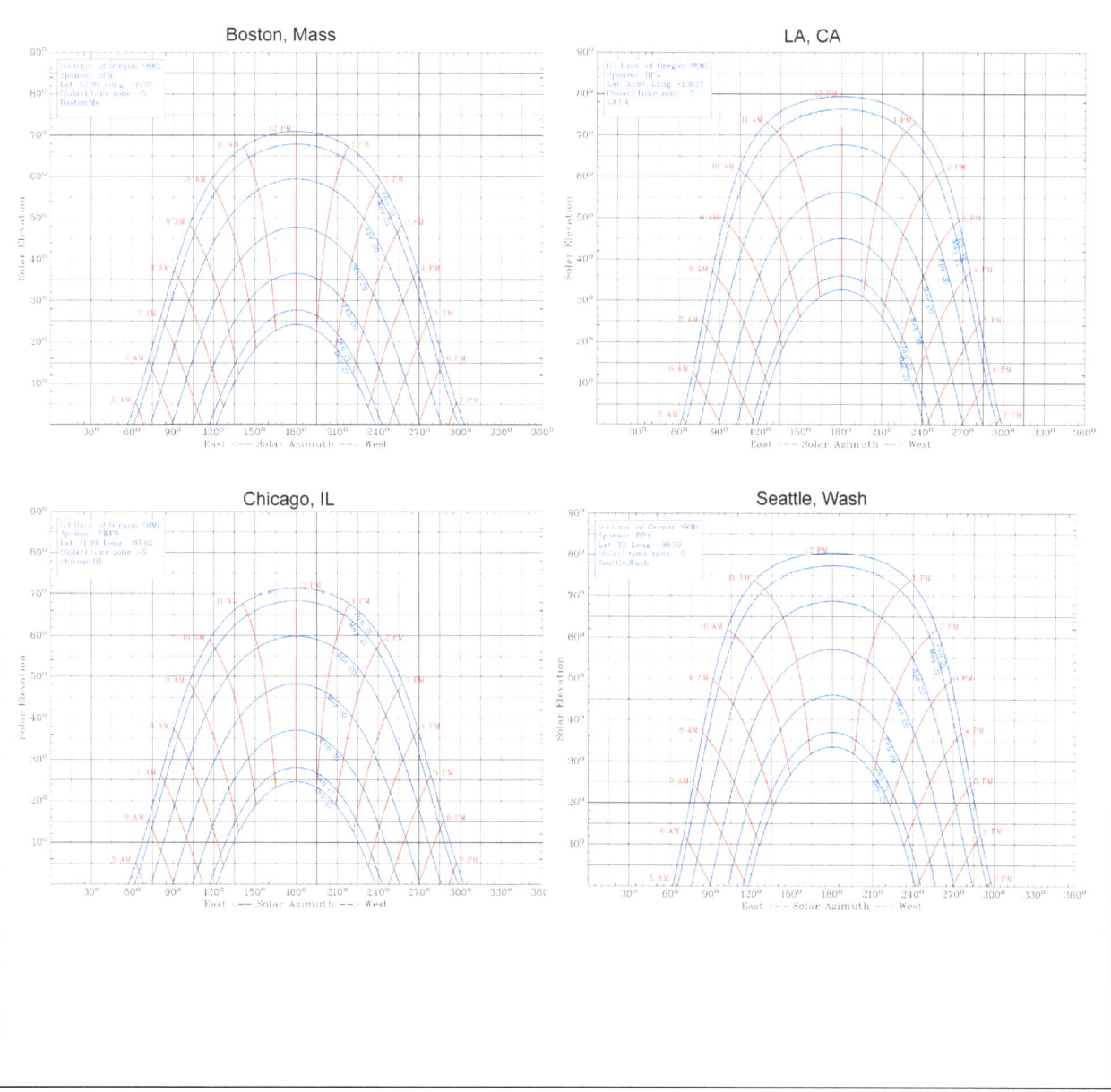

| 10 | <u>Maximum Availability Coincides with Peak Demand</u> | 10 |

Air conditioning is one of the heaviest loads a building can have, and during the summer, it's at its peak. So is Solar radiation! During the summer we get longer days, which give us more energy from the Sun.

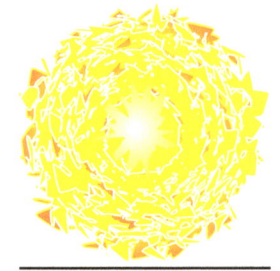

<u>Did You Know</u>

That you can eliminate 1000 pounds of CO_2 from the atmosphere by replacing one incandescent light bulb with a fluorescent bulb, and probably save around $100 over the life of that bulb?

<u>Really!</u>

Americans consume their body weight (150 pounds) in oil each week.

<u>Energy Facts</u>

America's dependency on foreign petroleum products is 58%.

<u>Do the Math</u>

For each mile a car drives, 1 pound of CO_2 is created
Typical lease gets 12,000 miles per year =
12,000 pounds of CO_2 per year for each leased car!

Magnetic Declination

Magnetic Declination Magnetic north is not true north! Below you will see another diagram of where magnetic north is with respect to true north. This information will be required to tweak your collector for better performance. You can interpolate your location from the value on the map below, or you can have NOAA Satellite and Information Services calculate it at http://www.ngdc.noaa.gov/geomagmodels/Declination.jsp where all you need is the zip code.

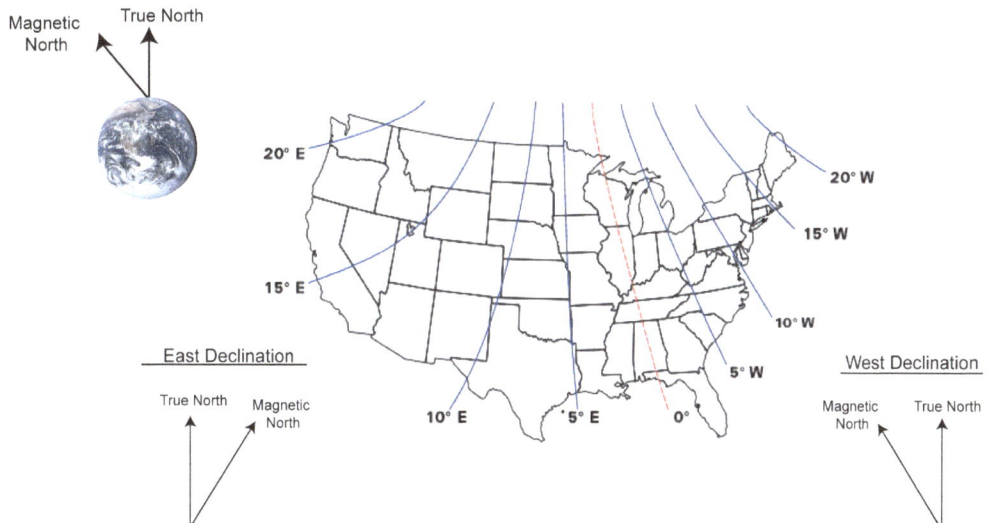

City	State	Magnetic Declination Face Collectors (south)
NYC	New York	13° West
LA	California	12° East
Chicago	Illinois	3° West
Houston	Texas	3° East
Philadelphia	Pennsylvania	12° West
Phoenix	Arizona	11° East
San Diego	California	12° East
Dallas	Texas	4° East
San Jose	California	14° East
Detroit	Michigan	7° West
Indianapolis	Indiana	4° West
Columbus	Ohio	5° West
Baltimore	Maryland	11° West
Memphis	Tennessee	3° West
Seattle	Washington	16° East
Portland	Oregon	16° East
Boston	Massachusetts	15° West
Denver	Colorado	8° East

11	**Less Vulnerable to Future Price Increases**	11

Having your own power supply on your roof can ease the pain when your electric utility announces a price increase. How often are you experiencing price increases from the electric company or your fuel company?

Did You Know
That we can generate electricity from the Sun by means of photovoltaic cells of all sizes and shapes?

Really!
An area 100 miles x 100 miles in the southwest United States has enough Solar energy to supply America with all its electrical requirements.

Energy Facts
The United States mined 5.3 billion tons of coal last year, and 75% went to generating electricity for the country.

Did you know
In most locations in the United States, property tax and sales tax are exempt from the sale of a Solar energy system?

Orientation

Orientation – orienting the Solar equipment to be used is very important to the outcome of the energy required for the "design intent" of your Solar system. Shading is Solar equipment's greatest enemy, so determining your location, free of shade, whether or not it is from trees or buildings next door (or even across the street) should be a priority. Being in the northern hemisphere, the Sun will always be on the southern horizon. All Solar energy equipment in the United States should be facing true south for the best Solar results. Don't forget to tweak your orientation with the magnetic declination factor.

A few definitions will assist your knowledge on orientation:
Angle is the angle of the collector with respect to the horizon. See diagram below.
Azimuth is the angle best described as the Sun's position from east to west (sunrise to sunset). See diagram below.

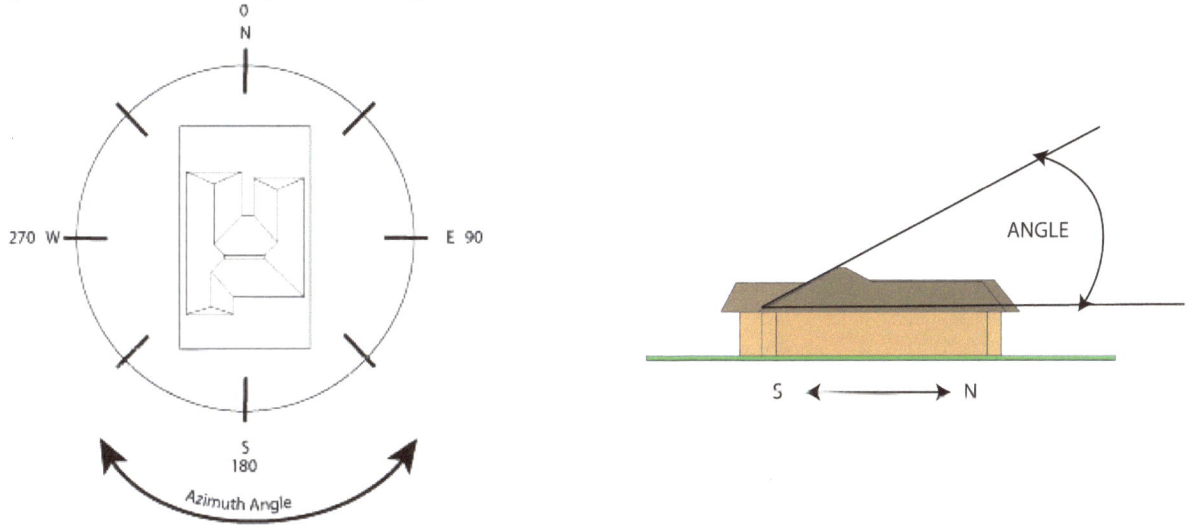

Optimum Orientation
If you are in the process of building a new residence:
The optimum angle orientation for **all year** use (domestic hot water) is the **latitude.**
The optimum angle orientation for **winter** (space heating) is **latitudes +15°.**
The optimum angle orientation for **summer** (AC) is **latitudes-15°.**
The optimum azimuth is directly **true south** (don't forget magnetic declination).

12	Independent	12

It is practical today to be energy independent. PV systems can be installed wherever there is Sunshine, and you do not have to be hooked up to the grid. Supplying your own power or heat makes you that much more independent. This applies to the United States also; the less energy we require from overseas, the more independent we become. America being energy independent is the only way.

Did You Know

1 kW equals 1000 W?
The average American household uses 1000 kW per month.

Really!

Coal is not a renewable energy source because it takes millions of years to create.

Energy Facts

Power Plants usually are running only 30 to 40% efficient!

Oil – a barrel of oil at 100% efficiency equates to 1700 kWh; at 35 to 40% you are left with 640-700 kWh.

Natural Gas – one cubic foot of natural gas at 100% efficiency equates to 0.2929 kWh; at 35 to 40% you are left with 0.1025 to 0.117 kWh per cubic foot.

Coal – a ton of coal at 100% efficiency equates to 7617 kWh; at 35 to 40% you are left with 2665-3046 kWh/ton.

Do the Math

A typical American household family using 1000 kWh/month will go through the following:

Oil-1.5 barrels per month
Natural Gas-1756 ft^3 per month
Coal-750 pounds per month

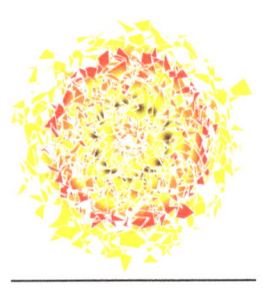  

Orientation – What About My House?

Up until now, we have been discussing the optimum orientation for Solar energy to work at its best. This information is best used by architects, site planners, or firms that have the ability to place the building any way on the lot they so desire. The best orientation is for your collectors or modules to be facing directly south. Since most homes are not built facing directly south, correction factors must be taken into consideration. The following chart will give the correction factor for your specific roof angle, and azimuth.

Angle Correction

0	14	18	37	45	59	90
flat	3/12	4/12	9/12	12/12	12/20	vertical
			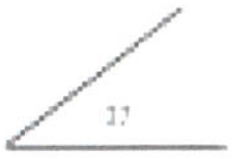	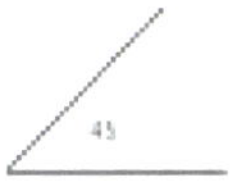	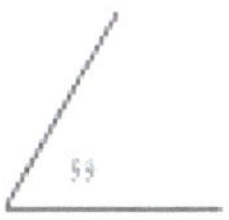	
86%	95%	97%	99%	99%	93%	75%

What is the azimuth angle of your building?
  a) Use a compass (remember to figure in magnetic deflection)
  b) Use your car's GPS system to get a proper direction
  c) www.GoogleEarth.com – this is a great tool you can get online for free. It will give you a picture of your building from space! All you have to do is enter an address, and within 3 seconds your building, with a bird's eye view, is on your screen. Go to the compass heading to see the azimuth angle.

Azimuth Correction

West	Southwest	South	South East	East
77%	94%	100%	93%	75%

These are general correction factors for the United States.
More detailed city correction factors can be found on page 85.

Examples
A home in NYC with a 14° angle, facing SW will receive
4.6 W/m^2 x 0.95(angle correction) x 0.94 (Azimuth correction) = 4.1 W/m^2.

A home in Denver, CO with a 12/20 pitch roof, facing west
5.5 W/m^2 x 0.93 x 0.77 = 3.93 W/m^2.

Solar Thermal Systems

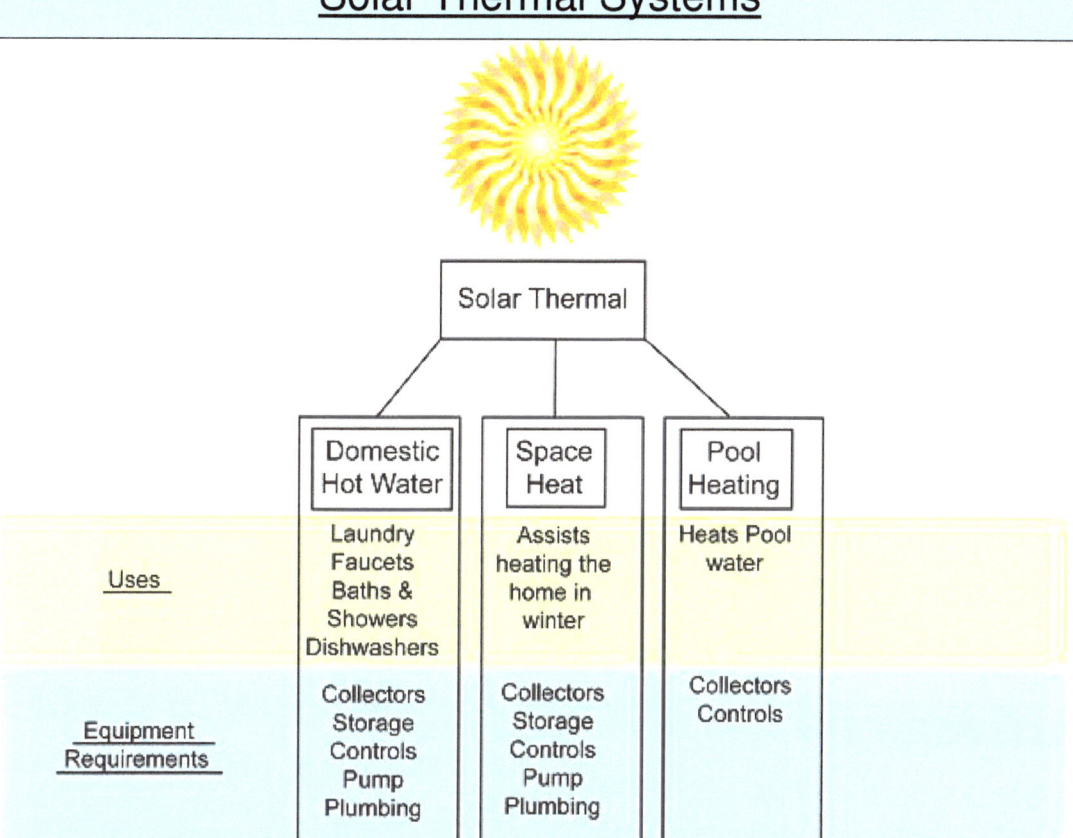

	Domestic Hot Water	Space Heat	Pool Heating
Uses	Laundry Faucets Baths & Showers Dishwashers	Assists heating the home in winter	Heats Pool water
Equipment Requirements	Collectors Storage Controls Pump Plumbing	Collectors Storage Controls Pump Plumbing	Collectors Controls

Collectors - captures the Sun's radiation and converts to thermal energy.
Storage - will store the Solar energy for later usage, with water being a prime candidate for storing this energy.
Controls - are the brains of the system and will operate the system unmanned as required.
Pump - circulates the fluid from the collector into the storage tank by means of a heat exchanger.
Plumbing - remainder of equipment to complete the installation of a Solar Thermal System: valves, check valves, thermometers, copper piping, to name a few.

I will be going into more detail on all of these items in the following pages

Good Candidate for Solar Thermal Energy
Southern exposure – best
Southwest/Southeast – good
East/West – not as good, but acceptable
Enough roof space
Sloped roof between 20°–60°
Will roof support extra weight?
Flat plate thermal collector 3-5 lb/ft^2
No Shading
Access to electrical panel and/or plumbing
Easy attic access (if mounting on a roof)

The Solar Advocate

13	Rugged	13

The average Solar thermal collector is made from aluminum, glass, and copper, which has very good life expectancy, and all with warrantees of 10 years or more. On the PV side, modules are made from glass and aluminum, which will carry a 25-year warranty. This equipment is designed for all weather conditions.

  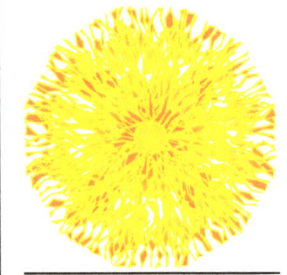

Did You Know

In one hour, more Sunshine falls on Earth than the entire world population will be using in one year?

Really!

New England has the highest oil usage, with 82% of New England households using oil as their main source of fuel.

Energy Facts

Emissions By State (million metric tons of CO_2 – 2008)
Texas – 625
California – 395
Pennsylvania – 284
Ohio – 274
Florida – 262
Illinois – 250
Indiana – 237
New York – 212

Do the Math

In 2008, 58% of all oil was imported.
This is up from 34% in 1973.

Types of Solar Thermal Systems

There are many types of Solar thermal systems on the market today to choose from. System choices will depend on local or regional weather conditions. The system will be affected by freezing conditions and high temperature conditions. A well-engineered Solar energy system will compensate for these conditions.

Basic Types of Solar Thermal Systems

Active – Requires outside power (electric, gas or any other type of fuel) to activate pumps and/or fans to circulate Solar heat to wherever it is required.

Passive – Passive systems rely on nature's Laws of Thermodynamics. By natural convection, heat is transferred from a collector to a storage medium, which is above the actual collector.

Direct – In a direct system, the water that you will be utilizing will be the water that goes through the collector. Whether it is the shower you took in the morning, or washing your hands before lunch, that water will have been directly heated by the collector.

Indirect – An indirect system will use a heat transfer fluid to transfer the heat from the collector into the storage tank. The fluid that goes through the collector will never be mixed with the water that's being utilized on demand. Propylene glycol is a very typical heat transfer fluid (non-toxic) that has been used recently, with very efficient heat transfer.

Solar Thermal Systems to be Discussed	Approximate Installed Price For Typical Solar DHW System
Batch Heaters or ICS (Integrated Collector Storage)	For the DIYer, less then $1000
Thermosyphon Systems	$3,000 – 6000
Drainback System	$5,000 – 7,500
Closed Loop Glycol System	$7,000 – 10,000

Take advantage of the **Prepackaged Solar Thermal Systems**. Over the past few years the Solar industry has been offering pre-packaged Solar thermal systems, which has made specifying and installing Solar that much quicker and more efficient. Prepackaged systems have the following qualities:

- Already engineered
- The majority of the system is pre-assembled
- Aesthetically pleasing
- Saves money
- Usually ships in one delivery
- Installations get quicker with time, reducing labor costs

14	**Constant**	14

At any given time, the Sun is radiating energy on 50% of the Earth. The Sun does not turn off, and have fun trying to shade. This radiating energy is in a form of electromagnetic radiation which is measured at Earth's outer atmosphere. Depending on the season, the Solar Constant for Earth is between 1300 and 1400 W/m^2. This energy is constant everywhere on Earth.

Did You Know

That back in 1447 Leonardo da Vinci was talking about Solar for industry using concave mirrors?

Really!

SRCC ratings are required for flat-plate collectors in order for consumers to take advantage of the federal tax break.

Energy Facts

In the past 10 years, the number of Solar thermal manufacturers has more than doubled, from 28 to over 65.

Really!

A flat-plate collector that has been certified by SRCC will be able to withstand ¾-inch hail at 60 mph.

Types of Thermal Collectors

The four most common types of Solar thermal collectors on the market today are:

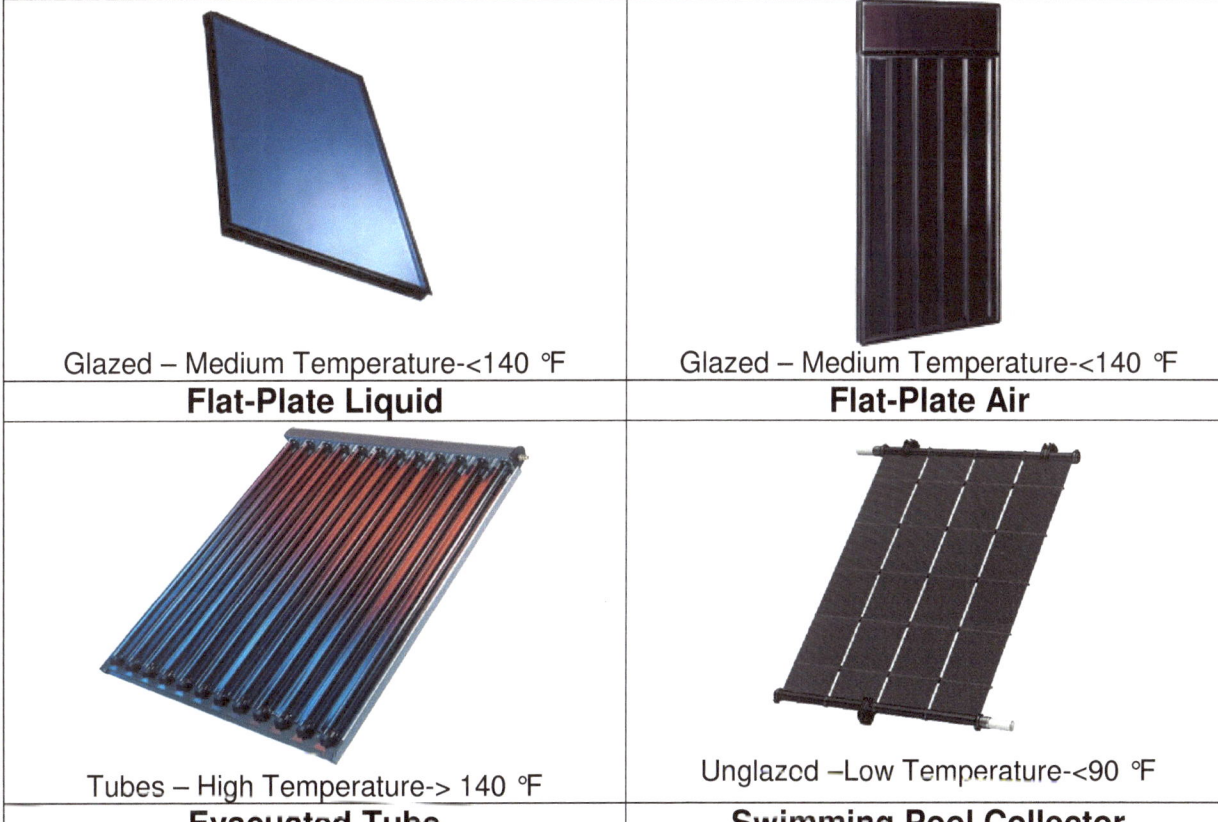

Glazed – Medium Temperature-<140 °F	Glazed – Medium Temperature-<140 °F
Flat-Plate Liquid	**Flat-Plate Air**
Tubes – High Temperature-> 140 °F	Unglazed –Low Temperature-<90 °F
Evacuated Tube	**Swimming Pool Collector**

FAQ (from the field)

How long will collectors last?

Most collectors are guaranteed by manufacturer for a minimum of 10 years.
With a good installation, a well-maintained system could last 25-30 years.

Do I need a new roof?

If you are planning to put a new roof up within the next five years, it is recommended that you put the roof up before you install the new Solar system. The collectors will protect your roof from the constant Solar radiation, which can substantially add to the roof's life expectancy.

How does shading affect my collectors?

Shading will affect the performance of any Solar thermal system! The more shading, the less performance from the system. Avoid all shading from the initial installation.

Will these thermal collectors work in the winter?

Solar thermal collectors work all year.

What are the effects of weather (rain, snow, hail, fog, wind)?

Solar thermal collectors are weather proof.

15	Universal	15

The same Sun that shines on the United States, shines all around the world. It does not discriminate at all.

Did You Know
That over 2 billion people in the world do not have electricity? Energy from the Sun will be the fastest-growing market for this population.

Really!
At the Atlanta Summer Olympics, the swimming pool was Solar heated.

Energy Facts
Saudi Arabia is the number one producer of oil at 16,665,000 barrels per day.
(The United States' consumption of oil is 20 million barrels of oil a day).

Do the Math   Pool Cover Economics

1000 square-foot pool, 80% natural gas efficiency, at $0.50 per therm		
78 ℉	**80 ℉**	**82 ℉**
New York (no cover) — $1448	$1904	$2384
With cover — $208	$296	$400
Denver (no cover) — $1757	$2120	$2408
With cover — $123	$168	$247
LA (no cover) — $1864	$2376	$2904
With cover — $168	$304	$472

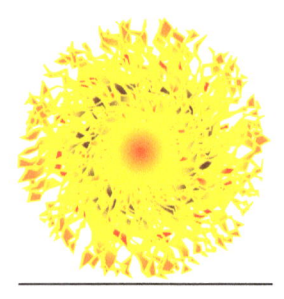  

Solar Pool Systems

Solar pool systems are increasingly becoming more popular because they:

- Work very well.
- Will save, if not eliminate, fuel costs.
- Will add at least one month before and after the season.
- Installs easily.
- Are the least expensive of the Solar thermal systems.

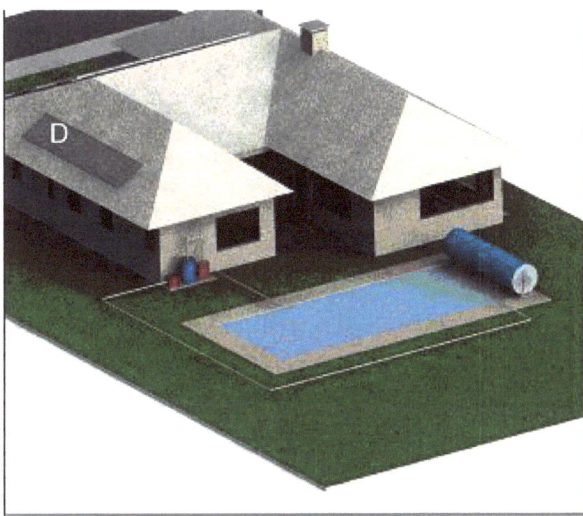

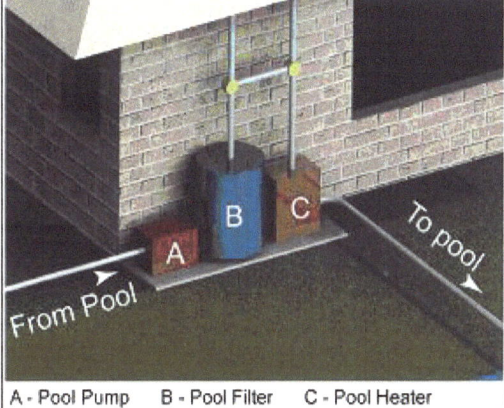

A - Pool Pump   B - Pool Filter   C - Pool Heater
D - Pool Collector   1 - Automatic Valve   2 - Automatic Valve

Swimming Pool Heat Losses
70% evaporation (potentially 2"/week)
10% ground – conduction
20% radiation from the sky

Importance of the Pool Cover
- Will prevent pool heat from escaping
- Will directly convert long wave solar energy to heat and add directly to pool
- Will reduce evaporation and in turn save water
- Will reduce chemical depletion
- Will reduce cleaning time
- Will cost between $0.30 and $0.50 a square foot

System Operation
1 - Pool system is turned on manually or automatically.
2 - Water will travel from pool thru pump (A), and then Filter (B).
3 - Sensor on Solar Collectors (D) will detect the temperature, and if warmer than the pool water temperature, Valve 1 is automatically open and allows pool water to travel through collector to add the Sun's energy. This is where the Sun's energy will increase the temperature of the pool water.
4 - From the collector, the water will travel through Valve 2, through the heater (the heater will go on only when required), and return to the pool.
5 - If pool collector is not warm enough to add to the pool water temperture, pool water will bypass collectors, and go from Filter (B) through Valve 1, then Valve 2, to the heater and finally back to the pool.

When designing a pool system, the designer wants to compensate for 95% of the heat losses from the surface of the pool. The square footage of the pool will be required to properly design the system. When sizing Solar pool systems, any range of 50 to 100% of the total pool surface area in Pool collectors are standard. Your location will be the deciding factor. In colder climates, close to 100% of the surface area in collector area will be used. In warmer climates, close to 50% can be used with significant results. If you are looking to reduce your fuel costs even further, use a cover. If this was not a Solar Energy book, I would recommend a pool cover before any Solar System. The combination of Solar pool collectors and a cover will reduce your fuel costs to a bare minimum, if any.

16	No Exploration, Extraction, or Transportation	16

Harnessing the Sun will reduce the need for any other energy sources. Local or regional power supplies will reduce the transportation of highly combustible fuels, reducing road wear and tear. Let's include all of those pipelines we have to dig up the Earth for.

Did You Know

Geothermal energy is stored Solar energy?

Really!

Running a full dishwasher versus doing the dishes by hand will save hot water. If you use an Energy Star dishwasher, you will surely reduce your hot water demand.

Energy Facts

The United States' natural gas reserves = 238 tcf.
The world's natural gas reserves = 6,254 tcf.

A Bit of history

In prehistoric times, caveman sought out south-facing caves to take advantage of the Sun's heat and light, and also protect against the northern wind.

Collectors – Flat-Plate Liquid

Flat Plate Collectors have been heating hot water for the past 75 years, if not longer. The design, engineering, and manufacturing have been getting better over the years and these advances are why I prefer FPC for domestic hot water heating.

A Flat Plate Collector will use a liquid, such as water (with no freezing conditions), or an "antifreeze" type of fluid, like propolyne glycol, to transfer the Sun's energy from the collector to the storage tank. Propylene Glycol is non-toxic and is being used in the food industry.

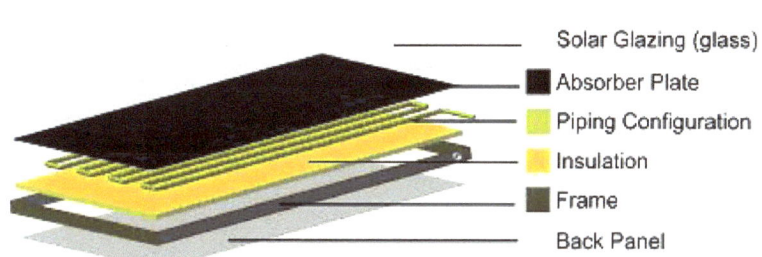

- Solar Glazing (glass)
- ■ Absorber Plate
- ■ Piping Configuration
- ■ Insulation
- ■ Frame
- Back Panel

Solar Glazing - The qualities you look for in glass for a flat plate collector are low iron and high transmittance. A minimum of 90% transmittance should be used. The average thickness of the glazing is between 0.13 inches and 0.2 inches

■ **Absorber Plate** - Absorber plates are normally a coated copper sheet. This coating is called a "selective surface", and will max the absorption of any of the Sun's energy, which will minimize emittance. A good selective surface will have an absorptivity of over 90% and an emittance of less than 10%.

■ **Piping Configuration** - Various types of piping configurations with some of the more common being:

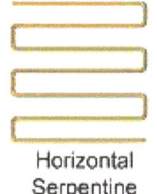

Header Riser   Horizontal Serpentine   Vertical Serpentine

Serpentine configurations are one continuous pipe and the chances of leaks are minimal. This is one of the qualities I favor. On the other hand, Vertical Serpentine will not drain by gravity, so this arrangement is usually confined to a closed loop DHW System.

■ **Insulation** - Will hold the heat inside the collector until required by the system. Mineral wool has been successful in flat plate collectors. Any insulating material that will not retain moisture will work better.

■ **Frame** - Aluminum is the champion in this arena. It is light, durable, resists rust, and is weatherproof. Flat plate collectors have recently added colors to the frame, which makes your Solar System that much more aesthetically pleasing.

■ **Back Panel** - Protects the flat plate collector from the underside. A good collector will use aluminum.

☐ **Gaskets** - Seals the collector, and protects from weather. EPDM are normally used for the gaskets

More Collector Info:
Size - The range of sizes can be from 24 square ft (6' x 4') to 40 square ft (4' x 10')
Weight - Typical weight of a flat plate collector is between 3-4 lb/ft^2 or 80 - 120 lb each.
Efficiency - A good flat plate collector will have an efficiency over 75%.
Maximum Collector Pressure must be known to design the pump accurately and efficiently.
Fluid Capacity - How much fluid the collector holds. Remember this will add to the weight of the collector and in turn add to the weight of the overall system.

| 17 | **Extended Pool Season** | 17 |

By utilizing Solar pool collectors, you can extend your pool season by at least a month. How would you like to be the first in your neighborhood to be enjoying the pool, a month before anybody else?

Did You Know

That the amount of Solar radiation falling on our atmosphere is approximately 1,366 W/m^2 and this is called the **Solar Constant?**

Really!

Installing PV on 25% of the land that America uses for railroad tracks will supply the United States with all the electricity it needs.

Energy Facts

In 2008, the United States consumed 23,000,000,000,000 ft^3 of natural gas		
Electric power generation	6.7 tcf	29%
Industrial	6.7	29%
Residential	4.9	21%
Commercial	3.1	13%
Leased plant fuel	1.3	6%
Pipeline	628 bcf (billion cubic feet)	2.7%
Vehicle	30.1	1%

Do the Math

70% of imported oil goes directly to the transportation sector.

Collectors – Evacuated Tube

Evacuated Tube technology has been around since the 1970s, and is a very popular means of capturing the Sun's energy. A heat pipe which is attached to the absorber plate, is surrounded by a glass tube. This area surrounding the heat pipe maintains a vacuum. It is this vacuum, that will reduce heat loss to the outside to a minimum, if any.

Evacuated Tube Collectors = ETC

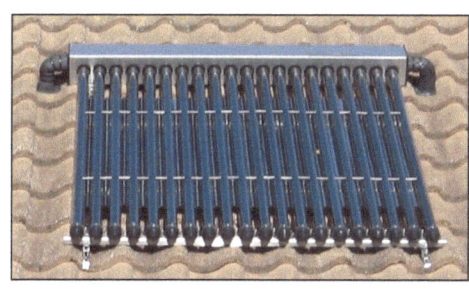

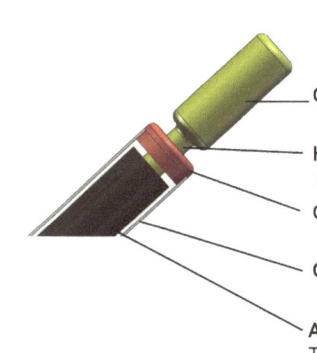

Condenser - gives off heat to a cooler fluid passing in the header.(not to scale)

Heat Pipe - transfers the heat from the bottom of the tube to the condenser. A good heat pipe will also have a vacuum.

Cap - responsible for keeping the seal, to maintain it's vacuum

Glass Cover - protects the absorber surface, and maintains the vacuum

Absorber Plate - absorber plates are normally a coated copper sheet. This coating is called a " selective surface ", and will max the absorption of any of the sun's energy, and will minimize emittance. The vacuum will minimize any heat to the outside.

Method of Operation
1 - Sun strikes ETC
2 - Sun's energy travels thru glass onto absorber
3 - Absorber transfer heat to copper heatpipe
4 - Because of the vacuum between glass and absober, theoretically there
    should be no heat loss.
5 - The heated heat pipe will "boil" the fluid in heat pipe, and transfer this energy
    by natural convection, to condenser, where it will give off it's energy to the passing
    fluid in the headers, and turn to a liquid, and then travel back down the heat pipe,
    only to start the process over again.

Advantages
Evacuated Tube Technology is tested and proven
Evacuated Tube Technology are more efficient in higher temperatures (>140F)
Better Evacuated Tubes have visual signs of cloudiness, to inform you when the
    evacuated tube has lost its vacuum. An ETC will work without a vacuum,
    but not nearly as well as with a vacuum.

Disadvantages
ETC could lose vacuum
Highly priced

18	Minimal Moving Parts	18

Anything that moves will break down eventually. Solar thermal systems have a pump or a fan as their only moving part. On a Solar PV system, the only moving part is a fan motor in the inverter box. What we're seeing more in the market are modules that do not require external inverter boxes, making these PV systems moving part-free!

Did You Know
That it takes just over eight minutes for Sunshine to reach the Earth? This is after the 1 million year process of convection from the core to the Sun's surface.

Really!
A five-minute shower uses about one third the amount of water and fuel as a bath. If you use a low-flow showerhead, you will get even better results.

Energy Facts
It's been over 50 years (late 50's) since the United States lost its self-sufficiency for oil.

Do the Math
Get an annual tune-up for your air conditioner, save 200 pounds of CO_2 emissions.
Get an annual tune-up on your furnace, save 640 pounds of CO_2 emissions.
Plug air leaks around doors and windows, save 750 pounds of CO_2 emissions per year.

Flat-Plate (FPC) Versus Evacuated Tube (ETC)

It was 1978 when I wrote my senior year Mechanical Engineering paper on <u>Heat Pipes Being Utilized in the Solar Energy Industry.</u> At the time, GE was the only company manufacturing evacuated tubes. It's now 30 years later and there must be over 100 companies manufacturing evacuated tube collectors (ETC). I have always liked and considered evacuated tubes, but there is a place for them. Over the past few years a growing question among consumers has been "Which collector is right for me?" Once again it comes down to the "design intent" of the project.

The key to the evacuated tube collector is the vacuum between the heat pipe and the outside glass cover. As of today, all evacuated tubes are made overseas, with the majority being manufactured in China. I have always questioned what the effect of traveling halfway around the world would have on the vacuum seal. Recently, evacuated tubes have a built-in "alarm" that will show a cloudy base when the vacuum has been lost.

Flat-plate collectors (FPC) for required temperatures less than 140 °F.
Evacuated tube collectors (ETC) for required temperatures more than 140 °F.

FPC $ < ETC $

My experience in New England & mid-Atlantic can give the following recommendations:

- **Solar Domestic Hot Water**-Under normal conditions, I would go with a flat-plate collector for domestic hot water. Reason being: most municipalities require mixing valves limiting the temperature of the hot water to be distributed to about 125° on all hot water systems. I do not need the extra temperature increase from evacuated tubes.
  Note – I would consider using evacuated tubes for DHW if I were placing my collectors in the east or west direction, for that extra kick of energy.
- **Solar Domestic Space Heating (low temperature)**-When designing low temperature radiant floor heating, I can still get away with a flat plate collector.
- **Solar Domestic Space Heating (retrofit)**-Depending on the type of system I am retrofitting, I would consider using evacuated tube. This is an area where I might require higher temperatures to match my existing system requirements.
- **Commercial Applications**-More inclined to use evacuated tube for any type of commercial application, again depending on the temperature required.

19	Abundant	19

The amount of Sunshine that falls on the United States each year is more than we will ever need or use.

Did You Know
That wind power is the fastest growing energy source in the United States? The wind in North Dakota alone can produce at least 30% of America's electrical energy requirements.

Really!
Approximately every 11 years the Sun reverses its overall magnetic polarity. North becomes south and vice versa.

Energy Facts
Each barrel of oil (42 gallons) will yield 19.7 gallons of gasoline (46% conversion), and each gallon of gasoline creates 20 pounds of CO_2.

Do the Math
The energy content of 3 gallons of oil equals 420,000 BTU

or

produce a 4' x 12' Solar pool collector from those 3 gallons of oil and you can generate
10 million BTU per year for at least 10 Years!

Collectors – Flat-Plate Air

Flat Plate Air Collectors will heat the air versus a liquid. Air collectors are not as common as a Flat Plate liquid collector, mainly because of performance. Air collectors recently have been used to add heat to localized areas in the building versus being part of a bigger air system. The system will work automatically, capturing the Sun's energy, converting it to heat, and distributing this heat to this localized area.

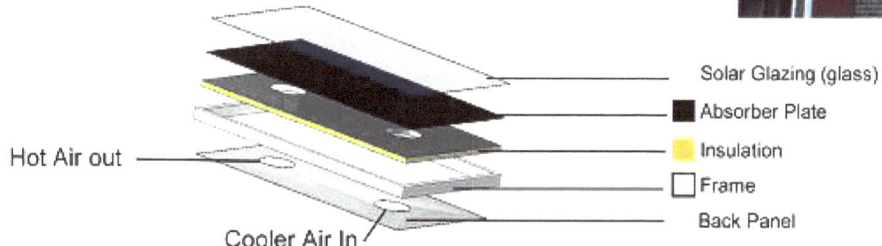

Solar Glazing (glass)
Absorber Plate
Insulation
Frame
Back Panel

Hot Air out
Cooler Air In

Solar Glazing - The qualities you look for in glass for a flat plate air collector are low iron and high transmittance. A minimum of 90% transmittance should be used. The average thickness of the glazing is between 0.13 inches and 0.2 inches.

Absorber Plate - Absorber plates are normally a coated copper sheet. This coating is called a "selective surface" and will max the absorption of any of the Sun's energy, and will minimize emittance. A good selective surface will have an absorptivity of over 90%, and an emittance of less than 10%.

Insulation - Will hold the heat inside the collector until required by the system. Mineral wool has been successful in flat plate collectors. Any insulating material that will not retain moisture will work better.

Frame - Aluminum is the champion in this arena. It is light, durable, resists rust, and is weatherproof.

Back Panel - Protects the flat plate collector from the underside. A good collector will use aluminum.

Gaskets - Seals the collector and protects it from weather. EPDM are normally used for the gaskets.

Because the angle of the Sun in the winter is so low, a collector that is designed for winter use can be installed vertically. In combination with an overhang, or awning (to block the summer Sun), the air collector will decrease your heat load for the building: the more collectors, the greater the savings. One of the advantages to the air collector working in this mode is that you can specify the local areas to be heated, versus depending on heating the entire building. In my travels, I have seen a 20' x 20' garage heated with 96 sq ft (3 - 4' x 8' air collectors). The customer likes to work on the weekends in his garage and now without a coat or gloves.

The Solar Advocate

We currently have full control over the Sun's energy to generate heat and electricity. We can use Solar cells to generate electricity for a device as small as a calculator, utilizing mini amps, to controlling a 1 MW power plant. The same thing goes for thermal; any size can be controlled.

Did You Know

That all communications satellites are powered by Solar energy?

Really!

Bad weather cost the world $130 billion in the first 11 months of 1998, and that was more than the years between 1980 and 1990 combined ($82 billion). Global warming?

Energy Facts

80 gallon electric hot water tank will use 5000 kWh per year.

100 gallon electric hot water tank will use 6200 kWh per year.

120 gallon electric hot water tank will use 7500 kWh per year.

Do the Math

The number of automobiles in the United States is 247,254,605

x 2 gallons of gasoline per day

x 20 pounds of CO_2 per gallon

4,945,092 tons of CO_2 enters the atmosphere every day in America.

SRCC – Solar Rating and Certification Corporation

SRCC is the organization that administers a certification, rating, and labeling program for Solar thermal collectors, and has another program for complete Solar domestic hot water systems. The two certifications that SRCC performs are as follows:

OG 100 – is the test for thermal collectors. In order to receive your **federal tax credit** for your Solar domestic hot water system, the collectors that you use must have OG 100 certification. An example of OG 100 results are given below. For a full list of certified thermal collectors, go to http://www.Solar-rating.org. This is where you'll find all data for all certified collectors for the United States. It's a place to do direct comparison of your collector with the competition.

OG 300 is the certification test for full Solar domestic hot water systems. OG 300 is not required by the federal government to be certified in order to get your tax rebate. Unfortunately, state governments are starting to recognize OG 300. You should verify with the installer or manufacturer if your system is OG 300 certified.

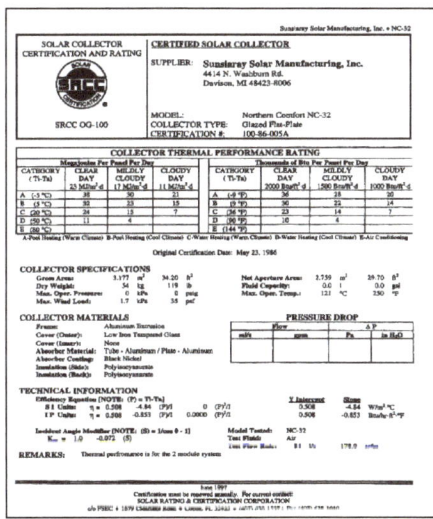

Actual SRCC Rating #'s			
Company	ft^2	1000 BTU/ panel/day	Weight (lb)
Flat Plate			
1	25	22.9	90
2	26	22.6	102
3	21	19	70
4	21	20.1	90
Tubes			
5	14.46	10.6	77
6	36.53	22.7	165
Pool			
7	47.44	0.9	20

Let's Compare a Flat-Plate Collector with an Evacuated Tube

Salesman 1 is selling me
3 #1 collectors for a total of 75 ft^2, 68.7 thousand BTU, and a weight of 270 lb.
What I should be looking at when the evacuated tube salesman hands me a quote:

To match Tube company 5

I would require 68.7/10.6 = 6.5 units; let's go with
6 Units for a total of 86.76 ft^2, 63.6 thousand BTU, and 462 lb or
7 Units for a total of 101 ft^2, 742 thousand BTU, and 539 lb.

To Match Tube company 6

I would require 68.7/22.7 = 3 Units
3 units for a total of 109 ft^2, 68.1 thousand BTU, and 495 lb.
Flat-plate wins this battle because of reduced square footage and weight at comparable performance.

| 21 | Lessen the Dependence on Fossil Fuel | 21 |

With today's Solar technology, at least 50% of our dependence on fossil fuel can be eliminated strictly from off-the-shelf items. As more people understand the availability of this equipment, our dependence of oil will be reduced to a minimum.

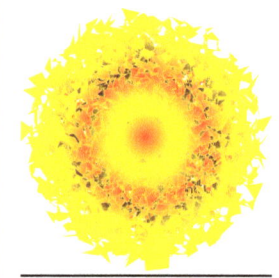

Did You Know

Off-the-shelf products are available today to generate a minimum of 50% energy savings for any home? This includes insulation, weatherproofing, conservation, and I have not started on the renewables…

Really!

52% of all residential households use natural gas as their primary fuel.

Energy Facts

2007 consumption of gasoline was 142,000,000,000 gallons.

A Bit of History

Romans invented glass, which improved the Solar energy situation for passive Solar design.

Collector Mounting

Solar Mounting

Tilt - Tilt mounting is the most common type of mounting for residential usage. Most Solar manufacturers of Solar collectors, or modules, will have a standard mounting package for their product. This will make the install easier, quicker, and get the install crew off the roof sooner. Take note, leave a few inches of space between the roof and PV module for air circulation, to keep module temperature down. PV's output decreases with temperature.

Flat Roof is the most common type of mounting for commercial applications.

Penetrating - Attaching the system to the roof will require ensuring that there will be no leaks! Use experienced commercial roofers for this task!

Ballasting - Add weight (cinderblock) to the mounting system. The higher the array angle, the heavier the load, the more Ballast weight will be required. A 31-pound module at 20° angle, inland, would require 40 pounds per square foot of module equalling 600 lb/module. Ballasted Thermal Systems are 3-4 times heavier. Because of this added weight, you will more likely need a structural engineer for a load analysis. On commercial buildings, most municipalities require this analysis to obtain permits.

Pole Mounted - Normally a rural application to pump water, electrify a fence, or light a sign. You'll surely be using concrete, so remember, you have a lead time for the concrete to cure. A trench will be required for the wires, so plan ahead! Pole Mounted Systems are the easiest way to convert to a Tracking System that can add as much as 35% increase in performance. See page 21 for your city's tracking increase.

Ground Mount is becoming more popular as you get out of suburbia and headed towards rural country. Note that all ground mount systems will have some type of trench to get your wires or plumbing to the desired location.

BIPV (Building Integrated PV) uses PV in the actual construction of the home. Example would be replacing the windows with see-through PV modules. Warning! Extremely expensive due to the custom nature! It could be three times more expensive then PV and the lead time is in months. Last I heard was that UL was required, which can add to cost, and planning.

The Solar Advocate

22	Increased Self Reliance	22

Americans have always prided themselves on self reliance. It's all part of taking care of oneself. We can handle our own energy problem right here in the United States without depending on any other country. With the amount of sunshine that hits the United States, especially the southwest, and the amount of wind that corridors the Midwest, there is no reason why we should not be self-reliant today.

Did You Know

That Germany is the leader in Solar energy around the world? That's ironic because the weather conditions in Germany are worse than Seattle or Syracuse.

Really!

Solar thermal systems collect about 45% of the Sun's energy and convert it to heat.
Solar electric systems collect 10% of the Sun's energy and convert it to electricity.

Energy Facts

In Texas, 0.43 gallons of water are consumed for each kilowatt produced. A single 100 W light bulb on for one year would use almost 375 gallons of water. A 10 kW Solar PV system, generating 14,000 kWh per year, will save 6200 gallons of water per year.

A Bit of History

Romans were the first to have enacted laws that would protect one from having their access to the Sun obscured or blocked.

54

Thermal Systems – Batch Heaters

Batch Solar Water Heaters are one of the simplest technologies in the Solar industry today. The collector and storage are combined into a single insulated enclosed box, covered by glass. This type of collector, is normally a Do-It-Yourself project and can be found more in a rural setting. Batch systems are passive and do not require any external power for pumps, fans, or controls. When hot water is needed, fresh water from the ground will be pre-heated by the Batch Solar System before it enters the conventional hot water heater.

Batch Solar Water Heater = ICS (Integrated Collector Storage)

Ground System

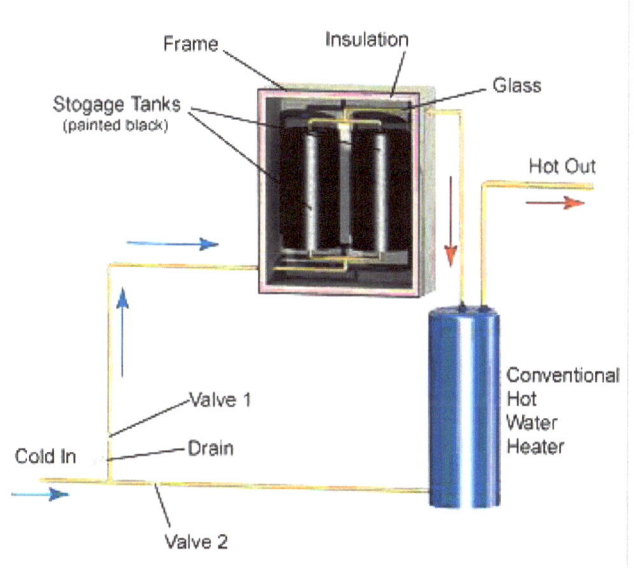

Roof System

Carport System

Method of Operation
- Hot water is demanded for shower, laundry, or dishwasher, etc.
- Fresh cold water enters the system.
- Meanwhile at the Collector, the Sun is continously heating the ICS, naturally forcing hot water to rise to the top of the tanks.
- Fresh cold water will push this hotter water into the conventional hot water tank, in turn reducing the amount of energy required to heat the requested water.

Winter Use
- Batch Solar Water Heaters can not be used in freezing conditions!
- The pipes to and from the ICS will freeze, and burst first, then the ICS unit will be damaged.
- In the winter, drain water from ICS (from drain), turn off valve 1, and turn on valve 2.

Advantages	Disadvantages
■ Very inexpensive to build	■ Does not work in freezing conditions
■ Minimal maintenance	■ Does not perform well in very hot climates
■ Easy install	■ Is not certified by SRCC (no Federal rebate)
■ A Do-It-Yourself project with dozens of plans online	■ Structure may not hold added weight
■ Passive - no external fuel required	■ Weekend plumber thinks he's a professional

23	Increased Local Economics	23

All Solar energy systems, whether thermal or electric, will require an installation team, sales team, and office staff. These are local jobs and will only improve local economics. You could be receiving parts locally or just getting a great sandwich at the local deli; either way you're leaving your money locally.

Did You Know

Homes can be heated both actively and passively by the Sun? An active system would require an outside energy source (electricity) to transfer the Sun's energy. A passive system can do it strictly by the building design and orientation.

Really!

In one second, the Sun releases more energy than mankind has used so far.

Energy Facts

Earth receives an equivalent amount of Sunshine in 20 days to replace our entire reserves of gas, oil, natural gas, and coal.

Do the Math

For each Therm burned, 11.9 lb of CO_2 enter the atmosphere.
56,286,013 homes in the United States are fueled by natural gas.

 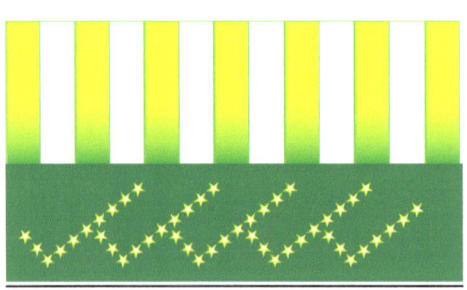 

Thermal Systems – Thermosyphon System

Thermosyphon Systems are another type of "passive" Solar system, that does not require an external source of fuel to operate. Hot water rises and cold water falls is the theory behind Thermosyphon Systems. These types of systems are very popular overseas, especially where freezing conditions do not exist. Thermosyphon Systems can use either a flat plate collector, or an evacuated tube to collect the Sun's energy. It is very important that the storage tank is above the collector to maintain this natural convection of heat.

Residential

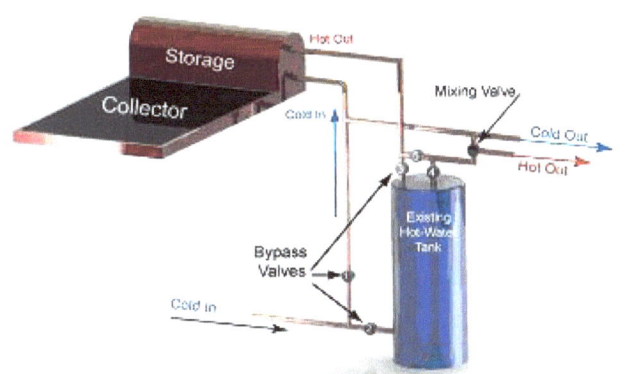

Apartments

Commercial

Method of Operation
- Hot water is demanded for shower, laundry, or dishwasher, etc.
- Fresh cold water enters the system.
- Meanwhile at the collector, the Sun is continously heating the FPC or ETC, naturally forcing hot water to rise to the storage tank above the collectors.
- Fresh cold water will push this hotter water into the conventional hot water tank, in turn, reducing the amount of energy required to heat water.

Winter Use
- Thermosyphon Systems can not be used in freezing conditions!
- The pipes to and from the Thermosyphon System will potentially freeze and burst. In the winter, drain water from Thermsyphon, turn off valve 1, 3, 5 and turn on valve 2.

Solar with No Backup
- Turn off valve 2, 3, 4.
- Cold water enters the system, travels through the Thermosyphon storage tank, travels through valve 5, goes through Mixing Valve, and finally hot water to house.
  Mixing Valve - will combine cold and hot water to desired output water temperature, and are required by law in most municipalities around the country.

Advantages	Disadvantages
■ One of the most common types of Solar DHW Systems	■ Does not work in freezing conditions
■ Minimal maintenance	■ Does not perform well in very hot climates
■ Easy install	■ Check SRCC for Certification (No Federal Rebate)
■ Can use flat plate collectors or evacuated tube	■ Structure may not hold added weight
■ Passive - no external fuel required	■ Storage tank must be above collectors

The Solar Advocate

24	Preserves Natural Resources	24

Solar energy does not require digging, strip mining, or even using the billions of gallons of fresh water to cool power plants. How many natural resources are we depleting looking for shale in the Rocky Mountains to be converted to oil?

Did You Know

That flat-plate collectors are the most commonly used equipment for Solar domestic hot water heating?

Really!

Taking a train to the Sun going 200 mph will take about 53 years.

Energy Facts

The average American home produces twice as much greenhouse gases as an average car.

Do the Math

Once installed, Solar energy systems have no variable costs.

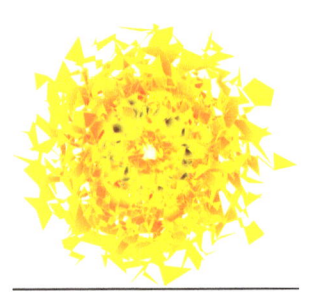  

Thermal Systems – Drainback

A Drainback System consists of collectors (Flat Plate or Evacuated Tube), storage tank, a small reservoir for the Drainback process, a heat exchanger (internal or external), controls, temperature sensors, and any additional plumbing. Essentially when the system is shutting down from either a filled satisfied tank, bad weather (rain or snow), night time, freezing conditions, or stagnation, the systems fluid (normally a mixture of 50% Propylene Glycol (non-toxic anti-freeze), and 50% water) will drain back into the reservoir. When these conditions are lifted, the Drainback system will operate once again. Because Drainback systems require gravity to operate, it is very important to have all pipes slope downward for proper drainage into the reservoir and the collector must be able to completely drain. One continuous tube collectors will not work for a Drainback system.

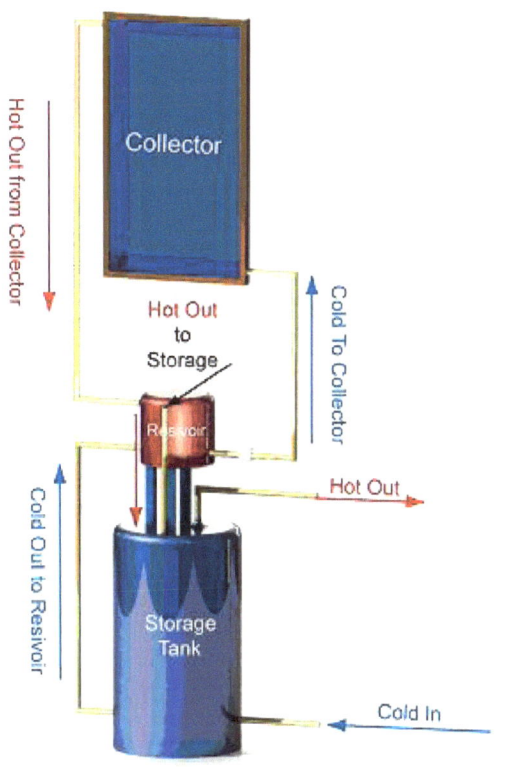

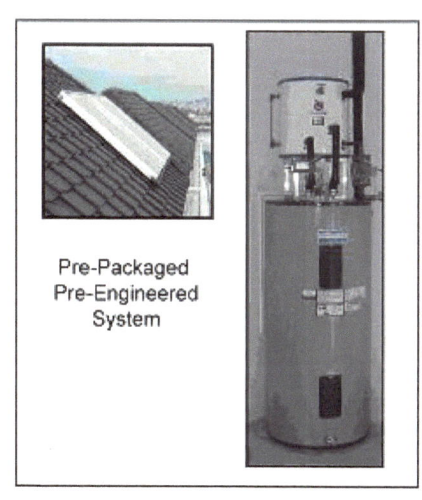

Pre-Packaged
Pre-Engineered
System

Advantages	Disadvantages
■ Perform very well all year	■ Need high head pumps for Collector/Reservoir circuit
■ Pre-engineered packages are available	■ Crucial that the pipes slope down for proper drainage
■ Safety features against freezing	■ Pumps could be loud
■ Safety features against stagnation	■ System could cycle on and off in the morning

25	**Strengthen Energy Security**	25

Our country's energy security is based on being independent of all external oil exporting countries. From a heating and electrical standpoint, I believe we have the necessary technology to be independent of these countries. It's the transportation sector that needs work.

Did You Know
In 1990, an aircraft made it across the United States strictly powered by Solar photovoltaics?

Really!
The Sun consists only of gas, no solids.

Energy Facts
The TV sets in the United States will use the equivalent energy of a nuclear power plant when turned off. See section on Phantom Loads, page 97.

Do the Math
Germany, Japan, the U.S., and Spain are leading the world in PV installations.

Thermal Systems – Closed Loop Glycol System

The **Closed Loop Glycol System** is a standard Solar Energy DHW (domestic hot water) System. A typical system contains collectors, a storage tank, controller, necessary plumbing ("Solar station"), and an existing hot water tank. This type of system will perform all year with no down time due to freezing in the winter or overheating in the summer. I personally have witnessed hundreds of these systems being installed and I am happy to report that my confidence in the Solar Closed Loop Glycol System remains extremely high!

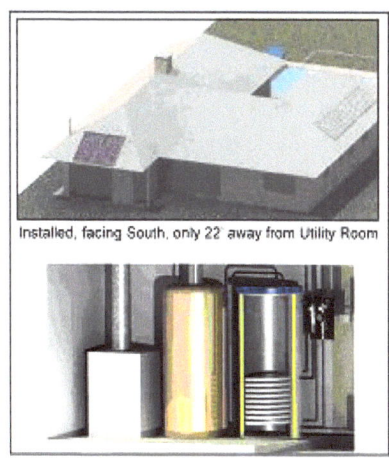

Installed, facing South, only 22' away from Utility Room

Collector - Captures the Sun's energy and converts it to heat and transfers heat to pumped Glycol Solution.

Controller - The "brains" of the system. With the help of two temperature sensors, when the temperature at the collector is 8-12 degrees hotter then the storage tank the controller will instruct the pump to start the system.

Pre-Assembled Plumbing "works" - Check valves, pumps, thermometers, pressure valves, etc. Sometimes called "Solar Station", "Energy Pack", or "Pumping Station."

Solar Storage Tank - Will store Solar pre-heated water before entering existing hot water tank.

Existing Hot Water Tank - Will back up your Solar system.

Propylene Glycol is a typical fluid used in Solar energy systems. It is non-toxic and will prevent the system from freezing and overheating. A 50% mixture of glycol and water is standard. Colder climates could require higher percentages of glycol in the mix.

Method of Operation

- Sun shines on collector, heats absorber plate, and transfers heat to Glycol mix.
- Controller measures at least an 8-12 degree increase of collector temperature over Storage Tank temperature and turns pump on to circulate Glycol Mix.
- Heated glycol mix travels through "Solar station" into the Solar tank's internal heat exchanger.
- Internal heat exchanger will release heat directly to the water in the Solar Storage Tank.
- Cooler glycol mix returns back to the collector through the Solar station.
- Process will continue until tank has reached its upper temperature limit (normally about 160°F), and then the controller will shut down the system.

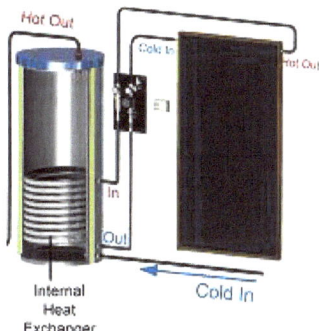

Internal Heat Exchanger

26 | Increase Value of Home | 26

Installed, working Solar energy equipment will increase the value of your home. Wells Fargo will add 20x one year of energy savings to the value of the home. If a Solar domestic hot water system is going to save you $100 per month, you have now increased the value of your home by $24,000.

Did You Know
The demand for Solar energy has increased by a minimum of 25% yearly over the last five years?

Really!
There are over 150 oil to gasoline refineries in the United States

Energy Facts
The capacity for a material to retain energy is called **Heat Capacity**.
water – 62.5 BTU/ft^3/°F
air – 0.018 BTU/ft^3/°F
This is why we use water for storage in Solar domestic hot water systems.

Do the Math
EPA says a 6 kW PV system in New Jersey will save
32 lb NO_2
44 lb SO_2
17,199 lb CO_2
from being dumped into our atmosphere per year.
17,199 pounds of CO_2 would require 2 acres of CO_2-absorbing trees.

Thermal Systems – Closed Loop Glycol System (2)

2 Tank System

2 Tank System will use two separate tanks for the system to operate.
#1 Tank - Solar storage tank will pre-heat the cold water entering the system and transfer it to the existing hot water tank.
#2 Tank - Existing Hot Water Tank will add any additional required energy to the pre-heated water coming from the solar storage tank.

2 Tank System will use 1 Internal Heat Exchanger or 1 External Heat Exchanger.

I prefer the **2 Tank System** over the **1 Tank System** because of it's ability to be independent. If installed properly, you will have the option to isolate each of the systems for maintenance and/or servicing.

1 Tank System

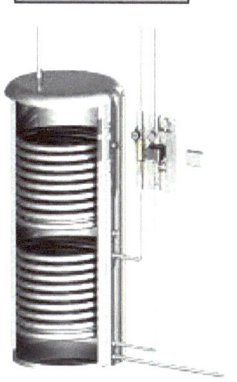

1 Tank System will use only one tank for both Solar and existing DHW.
Bottom Coil will be for Solar.
Top coil will be hooked up to your existing fuel source (gas, electric, or oil), and will supply additional energy that the Solar loop didn't supply. Top Coil is used as the back-up.

1 Tank System will have 2 Internal or 2 External exchangers

External Heat Exchanger

OG 300 requires a double wall heat-exchanger if using Glycol as a Heat Transfer Fluid. Unfortunately, Internal Heat exchanges do not fit in this category. External Heat Exchangers are accepted. OG 300 is not required for the federal rebate, but some states are following the OG 300 lead. Check with your installer. I prefer Internal Heat Exchangers because of their direct performance. Don't mistake OG 100 (collector certification) with OG 300 (system certification).

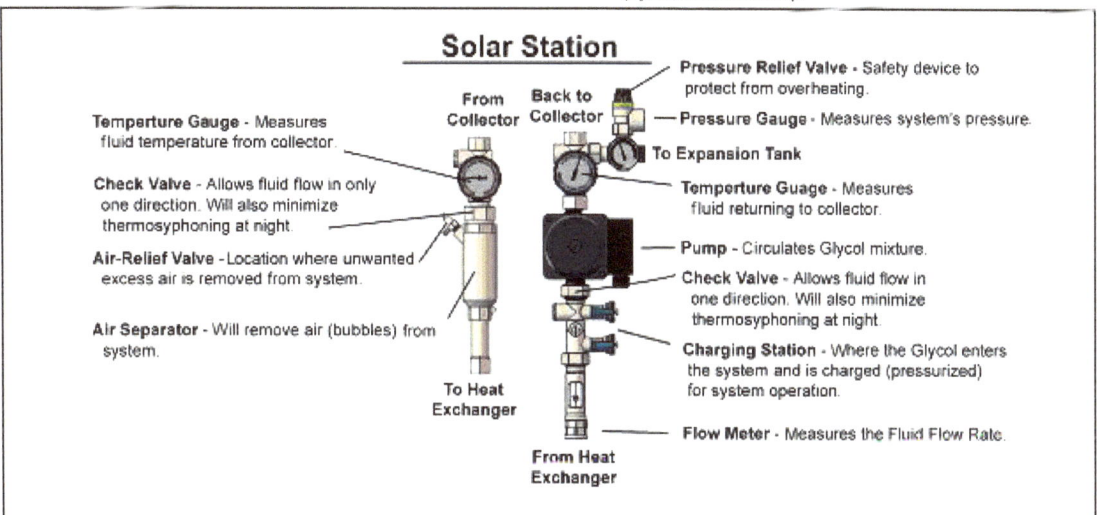

Solar Station

Temperture Gauge - Measures fluid temperature from collector.

Check Valve - Allows fluid flow in only one direction. Will also minimize thermosyphoning at night.

Air-Relief Valve - Location where unwanted excess air is removed from system.

Air Separator - Will remove air (bubbles) from system.

Pressure Relief Valve - Safety device to protect from overheating.

Pressure Gauge - Measures system's pressure.

To Expansion Tank

Temperture Guage - Measures fluid returning to collector.

Pump - Circulates Glycol mixture.

Check Valve - Allows fluid flow in one direction. Will also minimize thermosyphoning at night.

Charging Station - Where the Glycol enters the system and is charged (pressurized) for system operation.

Flow Meter - Measures the Fluid Flow Rate.

The Solar Advocate

The fuel from the Sun is automatically turned into heat or electricity depending on the type of collection system being used. Oil, gas, coal, or wood must be burned to acquire its energy. Did I mention that oil, gas, coal, and wood systems all require chimneys?

Did You Know
That Solar powered traffic signs have replaced the battery packs with PV panels?

Really!
In the typical American home, 64% of electricity is used for appliances. Refrigerator with the most (14%), followed by lighting (9%).

Energy Facts
In 2007, 142.4 billion gallons of gasoline were consumed in the United States
x 20 lb CO_2/gallon, equals
2,848,000,000,000 lb CO_2 in the air.

A Bit of History
During the French Revolution, Antoine Lavoisier developed a Solar furnace capable of 3000 °F. He lost his head to the guillotine before going to market.

 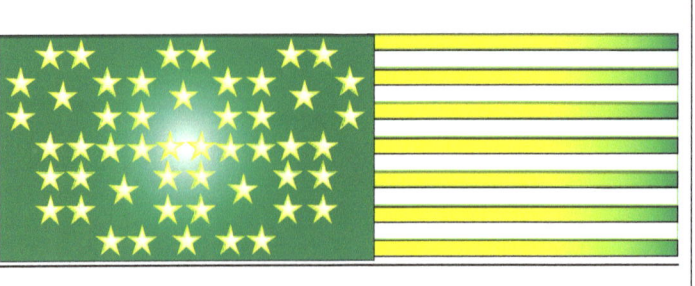 

Sizing Solar DHW

When we are talking about Solar DHW, we are referring to hot water for showers, dishwashers, and laundry. How much water does your family use? With the average American using approximately 20-30 gallons per day, a typical family of four will use approximately 80-120 gallons per day of hot water.

The **Rule of Thumb** for sizing Solar thermal is 20 ft^2 of collector area for the first two individuals, with between 8 (Southern U.S.) and 14 (Northern U.S.) ft^2 of collector for all additional family members.

The **Rule of Thumb** for storage tanks would be 1-1.5 gallons per square foot of collector area. According to these rules I am looking for approximately 60-75 ft^2 of collector area and a storage tank approximately 75-120 gallons.

Working out of the mid-Atlantic and New England regions, I use the following chart to achieve the initial design intent of a **Solar Fraction** of approximately 75%.

# of People	# of collectors	Gallons of storage
1-2	2	80
3-5	3	100
5+	4	120 (119)
I would use this chart for the vast majority of the U.S.		

Your Solar installer will tweak these #'s to <u>YOUR</u> design intent and equipment availability. Roof space, orientation, and available room for storage tanks will all be part of this final decision on the system size that will best suit your family's needs.

New Generation of Solar DHW Systems

Advancement in the Solar DHW industry has brought us full pre-engineered systems ready to be installed with no additional engineering design work. This advancement has saved on design and installation time. This new generation has also included multi-speed and variable speed pumps enabling the customer to add an additional collector while maintaining the most efficient flow rate for your system. Your local installer will assist you with your selection.

28	Infrastructure Reliability	28

By keeping your Solar thermal or PV system local (on your roof), you are reducing wear and tear on the existing infrastructure. Less wear and tear means more reliability to the entire system.

Did You Know
That our entire natural gas, oil, and coal reserve is less than three weeks of sunlight?

Really!
Typical gas heaters have an efficiency of only 50 to 65%
(35 to 50% go right up the chimney).

Energy Facts
Between late 1880s and 1940s, a Solar hot water boom took place from California to Florida!
California – 25,000 Solar domestic hot water heaters installed.
Florida – 60,000 Solar domestic hot water heaters installed.

Do the Math
Attention New England: for each gallon of oil used, 20 lb of CO_2 are emitted to the atmosphere. At a typical efficiency of 60%, let's increase to 35 lb CO_2/gallon of oil. Did I mention that 8.5 million households use oil as main source of fuel?

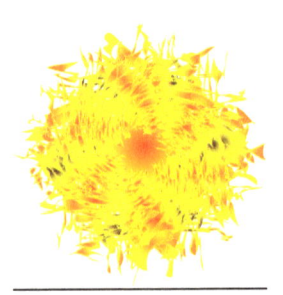 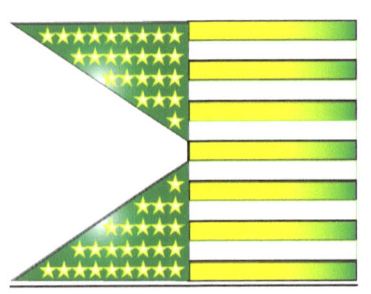 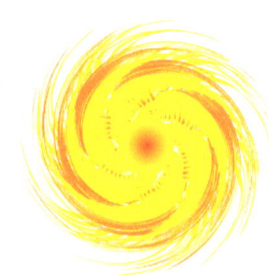

Instantaneous Hot Water Heaters

Instantaneous hot water heaters will provide hot water only as you need it. It does not have a storage tank where you will have continuous heat loss, it just makes hot water as you need it. Think about that space saved. These units can run with gas, electric, or oil. Gas units (80 to 90% efficient) have the best ratings, with electric (100% efficient) following. It is a perfect backup source for Solar domestic hot water systems.

In selecting an instantaneous hot water heater you will need to know the maximum amount of hot water that you will require.

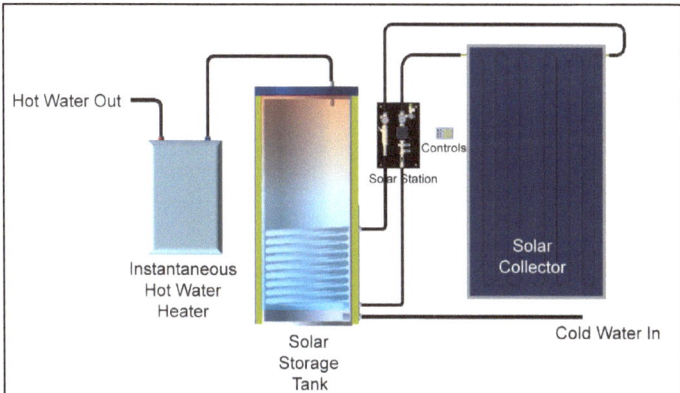

- **Faucets** 0.75 gallons to 2.5 gallons per minute
- **Low flow shower heads** 1.2 to 2 gallons per minute
- **Older Showerheads** 2.5 to 3.5 gallons per minute
- **Clothes washers** 1 to 2 gallons per minute

Depending on how much water you use and how your Solar energy system is functioning, instantaneous hot water heaters have a payback of 3 to 5 years. With a life expectancy of over 25 years and installation done in less than a day, the instantaneous hot water heater is the perfect choice for backup when using Solar domestic hot water heaters.

Advantages
Long term energy savings
Requires less space than the conventional hot water heater
Risk of water damage will be reduced
Continuous, unlimited hot water

Disadvantages
More expensive than a conventional hot water heater
It takes a minute or two to start up
Minimum water pressure is required
Gas, electric, and oil are the fuels to be used

The Solar Advocate

When we do not have to go to war to acquire our energy needs, our national security will be improved and secure.

Did You Know
That Solar powered buoys floating in the ocean are assuring nautical safety?

Really!
Solar domestic hot water is being used in over 3 million homes in Japan.

Energy Facts
Air conditioning should maintain 78 °F
For each degree lower you can add 6% to your electric bill.
At 75 °F, an 18% increase in electricity and
at 72 °F, a 36% increase in electricity.

Do the Math
The United States consumes 20,680,000 barrels of oil per day.
The United States consumes 9,286,000 barrels of gasoline per day.

 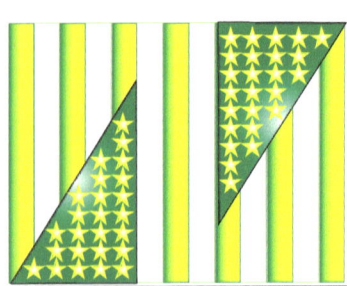 

Solar Space Heating

Up until now, we have been heating water for DHW. Space heating can also utilize Solar Energy in the same way DHW does. The only difference between domestic hot water systems and space heating systems is the size. In both cases, we are collecting energy at the collectors on the roof and transferring it to a storage tank for later use, whether it is to take a shower or run a small fan coil unit to heat the room. An important question you might want to ask yourself if you are considering space heat:

What Am I Going to Do With the Heat in the Summer Time?
Do I have a pool or a Jacuzzi to dump the heat? Are my kids coming home from college during the summer to use more hot water from our Solar domestic hot water system? Seriously think about dumping six months of heat.

New construction: If you are building from the ground up, your choices to utilize Solar thermal energy are numerous. Low temperature radiant floor heat, modular fan coil units, or basic baseboard heating can be used to heat a home with Solar energy.

Using Solar passive design elements, along with a well-insulated building (including windows and doors), can greatly assist the performance of your Solar space heating system.

Retrofit: If you are going to be adding to your existing heating system, it is recommended that you bring in the original contractor who put the system in, or at least have a consultation. The reason for this is that most Solar installers do not know HVAC equipment & controls as well as the original contractor. My biggest concern for retrofit space heating systems is the logic on how the Solar system will work in conjunction with your conventional backup system. Use caution when hooking up a Solar system to an existing HVAC system. <u>Have an experienced installer for the Solar space heating system.</u>

For this reason, I have been recommending that a customer goes modular. I have been successful for the past several years with fulfilling customer requests for Solar space heat by installing another domestic hot water system that will be hooked up to a fan coil unit that is strategically placed in the home to maximize your heating requirements. And because Solar energy is modular, I can keep on adding systems in the future.

The Solar Advocate

In 2009, the United States has a choice in selecting their energy source. With the price of fuel escalating the way it is, Solar domestic hot water is now a choice, and not an expensive alternative. I would like to say that it is an "appliance." PV is still expensive, but a very viable choice.

  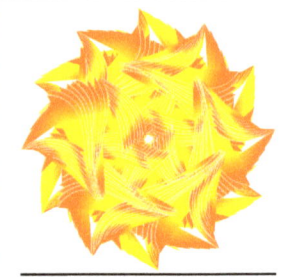

Did You Know
That the Energy Bill of 2008 will assure Americans that we will receive tax credits for photovoltaic and Solar thermal space heating and Solar domestic hot water systems for the next eight years?

Really!
8 tons of recycled aluminum is equivalent to 10,350 gallons of gasoline, which equals 86,067 kWh, which equals eight years of electricity for the average American household.

Energy Facts
The average Solar radiation received in the United States is between 3 and 9 kWh/m^2/day. At 15% efficiency, this equates to 0.45-1.35 kWh/m^2/day.

Do the Math
Supplying 1 million homes with Solar can reduce CO_2 emissions by 4.3 million tons a year, which is equal to removing 850,000 cars from the road.

Thermal Installation

You've heard the sales talk, you've selected the system that you're comfortable with, you've signed a contract, and now it's time to install.

Get Permitted!!!
Local and State Building Codes and Regulations
- Provides safety standards
- Without it, contractors can get into legal problems, and it would be almost impossible to take legal action if your system has problems.
- Will remove legal liability if someone is hurt.
- Rebates and most warranties depend on it.
    ### It's the Law

Thermal Installation
- Is the correct equipment at the job site?
- Is the area to be worked in clean, free of clutter and safe to work in?
- Did you get the permits?
- Were you informed about the estimated time to install?
- What is the sequence of the installation?
- Are you in agreement over where the collectors will be placed?
- Any shading that was missed in the initial visit?
- Are you in agreement with the piping and/or wiring layout?
- How are you getting the collectors up to the roof?
- Does installer have up-to-date license?
- Does installer have a plan to connect to existing equipment?
- Is the proper testing done?
- Does the system work?
- Was the area left clean?
- Were you informed on how the system operates?
- Did you receive a homeowner's manual?
- Did you receive emergency service numbers?
- Are you happy?
- Do you trust these guys?

31	High Value Jobs	31

Licensed plumbers, licensed electricians and licensed roofers are some of the occupations that are required in the installation of Solar equipment. Licensed occupations always get paid more than minimum wage.

Did You Know

That our seasons are caused by the Earth's 23.5° tilt?

Really!

Helios and Apollo were Greek deities of the Sun.

Energy Facts

Additional Professional Solar Jobs

■ Engineers	Design systems
■ Scientists	Come up with new and better materials
■ Project manager	Installation
■ Architects	Design new homes and systems
■ Builders	Installation
■ Planners	Come up with comprehensive plan
■ Educators	Teach for the future Solar industry
■ Sales	The seller
■ Entrepreneur	The people attempting financial success
■ Skilled labor	Plumbers, electricians, roofers, etc.
■ Financier	Getting the right financial package together
■ Investor	Getting the product or company on its feet

Equipment Maintenance

Maintenance for Solar energy systems, whether for thermal or PV, is really simple. If the system was designed and installed properly, the only maintenance required would be to keep the collectors or modules clean. Keep an eye on the collector or

module to see if there is any fogging, delaminating, warping, or any water leaks. If so, contact your installer. If all looks good, rinse off your modules periodically to keep all dirt and dust off the modules. This task should be done as required. Any tree growth since the installation of your system? Do you have to cut back on some of the growth? Remember PV hates shade! Periodically, it is advisable just to check out the system as a whole and report back to your installer for anything that doesn't look right (such as loose or exposed wires). Also check for animals that find it very comfortable to live underneath your collector array.

For closed-loop Solar thermal DHW systems, be prepared to do a litmus test on the fluid at least every three years. We are looking to keep the fluid neutral and not acidic.

Like I said, very simple.

32 Solar Surveys 32

Survey after survey shows that Solar energy will be this country's future energy source. With the price of fuel increasing the way it is, Solar is becoming an everyday vocabulary word for many Americans.

Did You Know

That Solar energy can reduce our trade debt?

Really!

Solar thermal collectors or PV modules will not destroy your roof. If anything, it will be protected from light, heat, and weather.

Energy Facts

A light tube will replace three 100 watt light bulbs.
In 8 hours per day, you can save $0.48, and
after a year you can save around $175, every year.

A Bit of History

As early as 400 BC, the Greeks were utilizing passive Solar design in their homes.

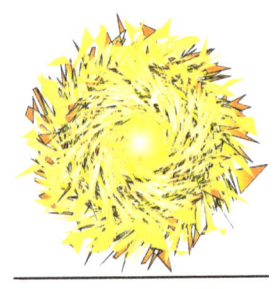 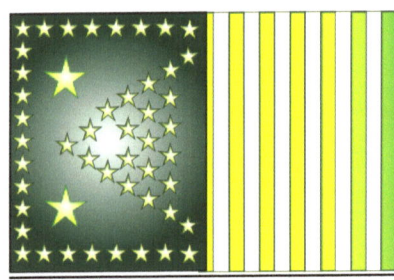 

Passive Design

Throughout time, man has used passive design to keep the family warm and cool throughout the year. Passive design is pure logic! When you need the Sun, let it in. When you have too much Sun, block it from getting into the building with shades or an awning.

Solar heating is done by natural means of radiation, convection, and conduction. There is no mechanical equipment assisting the Solar heating; instead, the building structure and orientation are designed for maximum Solar gain.

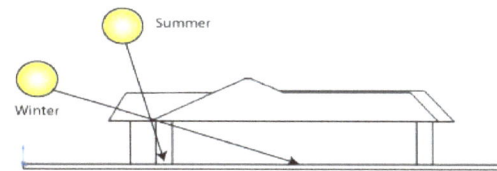

Overhangs on the south side of my home (pictured at the right) has brought the Sun into my home in the winter time, and shaded the Sun during the summer. In combination with a full house fan, we rarely use air conditioning in the summer. One of my neighbors, who does not have awnings on the south side of his home, was recently complaining about his high electric bill for all the air-conditioning he is using. I informed him that a set of awnings would probably reduce his cooling bill by half.

Rules of Thumb

◼ The building should be elongated along the east-west access.
◼ For optimum Solar heat gain the south face should receive the Sun between 9am and 3pm unobstructed.
◼ Rooms that required the most heating, cooling, or light should be on the south side of the building.
◼ Open floor plans optimize the use of passive energy.
◼ Shade the summer Sun with proper awnings or overhangs.
◼ Strategically incorporate thermal mass (water or stone).

__Direct Gain__ uses the Sun directly for heat. Sun enters the building, converts to heat and it is now being used by the residence to warm the space.

__Indirect Gain__ is the energy you receive from the mass that you are storing your passive energy in.

__Isolated Gain__ means energy entering a specific area (greenhouse or sunroom) can then be relocated later for your energy requirements.

33	**Modular**	33

With Solar energy you do not have to install all of the equipment at one time. Solar is modular and can be put up in phases. An example:

Phase 1 – Solar domestic hot water

Phase 2 – Solar space heating

Phase 3 – add more space heating, or go with PV

Did You Know

That due to the 23° tilt of the Earth, the Solar radiation intensity will vary by season? At a latitude of 45°, the intensity could vary from 92% in the summer to 38% in the winter.

Really!

PV modules convert Sunlight directly into electricity!

It's like magic!

Energy Facts

Hydropower is the most significant renewable energy source in America.

Do the Math

In 2008, electric power plants emitted:

9,042 thousand metric tons of SO_2

3,650 thousand metric tons of NO

2,516,580 thousand metric tons of CO_2

 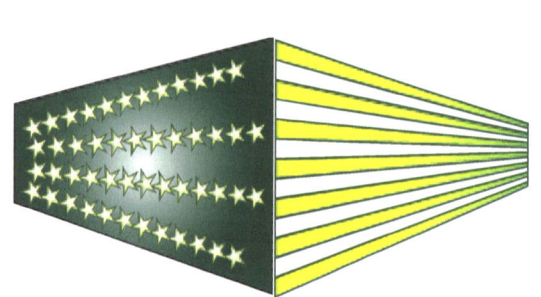 

Agricultural Solar Uses

Solar energy can generate electricity and heat anywhere there is Sun!

Solar
Domestic Hot Water
Space Heat

Solar
Water-Pumping

Solar
Crop Drying

Solarized
Electric fence

Solar Greenhouse

Solar
Crop Drying

Corn Crops To PV Farm

Solarized Insect Killer

Solarizing
Dish

Getting ready to install
Solar PV

The Solar Advocate

The Solar radiation from the Sun is the same during the summer, spring, fall, and winter. Its electromagnetic energy does not vary.

Did You Know
That Edmond Becquerel, in 1839, observed that sunlight was being absorbed by certain materials and can produce a small amount of electricity?

Really!
For every degree you turn down your thermostat, you can save up to 3% of your fuel bill!

Energy Facts
Coal being mined today was formed over 300 million years ago, the same as oil.

Do the Math

247 million vehicles in the United States:

136 million cars
110 million trucks
1 million busses

Solar Thermal Power Plants

Sierra SunTower will produce 5 MW of electricity powering up to 4,000 homes.

110 MW Florida

64 MW Nevada

553MW Mohave Desert

50 MW Mohave Desert

280 MW Arizona

Solar PV Power Plants

Large PV Power Plants

El Dorado, NV 10MW

Alamosa, CO 8.2 MW

10 MW going up in Chicago's South Side

Denver International Airport 3 MW

Nellis Air-Force Base 14 MW

PV = Photovoltaics

Photovoltaics generate DC electricity directly from the Sun.

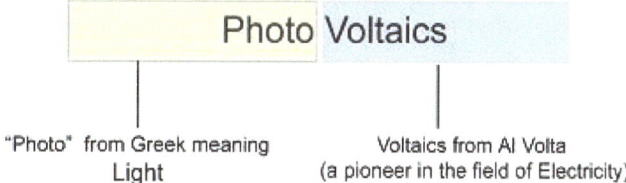

"Photo" from Greek meaning
Light

Voltaics from Al Volta
(a pioneer in the field of Electricity)

DC = Direct Current - electricity similar to batteries.
AC= Alternating Current - electricity that comes into your house through the outlets from the utility company.

In 2008, the installed World capacity of PV was 15,221 MW
and that's a 48% increase every 2 years for the past 10 years.

California is planning the installation of 3 Gigawatts of PV power by 2017
3,000,000,000 W / 200 W PV panels = 15,000,000 modules to be installed!
Thank You Governor Schwarzenegger!

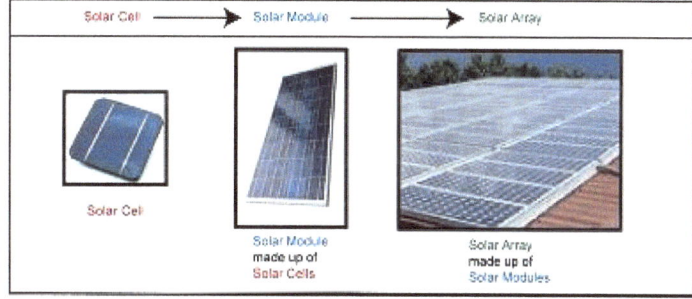

Solar Cell → Solar Module → Solar Array

Solar Cell

Solar Module
made up of
Solar Cells

Solar Array
made up of
Solar Modules

Good Candidate for Solar PV
Southern Exposure – best
Southwest/Southeast – good
East/West -- not as good, but acceptable

Enough roof space

No shading

Sloped roof between 20° - 60°

Will roof support extra weight?
PV modules 2-3 lb/ft^2

Easy access to electrical panel

Easy attic access (if mounting on roofs)

The Solar Advocate

35	Great Conversation Piece	35

With the dozens of PV and thermal installations I have assisted, somebody will always walk up to the crew to find out what's going on. The conversation normally ends up with the homeowner, and many times a sales appointment will be made.

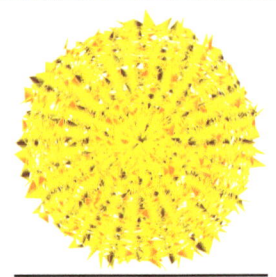

Did You Know

That a Solar domestic hot water system that costs around $8000 will cost about $2.20 per day over the course of 10 years? Yesterday's cappuccino cost me $3.45.

Really!

Solar energy can power anything that requires electricity.

Energy Facts

Emissions from an electric hot water system equals a midsize car going 12,000 miles at 22 miles per gallon, and that equates to 11 barrels per year.

Do the Math

A 10 kW PV system in New York will offset per year:

15 pounds of NO_2

37.9 pounds of SO_2

10.2 tons of CO_2

and that is equivalent to 1056 gallons of gasoline, or 386 barbecue propane tanks.

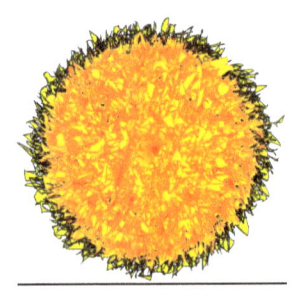
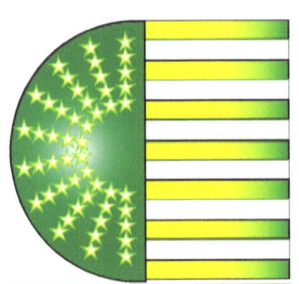

PV Applications

Photovoltaics generate electricity from the Sun. After the DC power is converted to AC power through means of the inverter, you have the same electricity that comes out of your electrical outlet.

The Sun can run anything, or everything, that requires electricity!

From

Calculators

PV
Applications

To

Power Plants

Some of the infinite PV applications:
Residential, commercial, and agricultural electrical requirements
Lighting
Water pumping
Traffic lights
Construction signs
Communication
Remote site power supply
Disaster relief applications
Consumer (gadgets)
BIPV (building integrated photovoltaic)
Standalone devices (parking meters, telephones)
Gate openers
Electric fences
Water-tank de-icers
Anything That Runs on Electricity

36	**Minimal Cost After Installation**	36

Once installed, Solar energy equipment requires minimal cost. A service call once every two years is recommended, and if your system is working properly, there should be no additional costs.

Did You Know
That PV modules only have an efficiency of around 12 to 18%?

Really!
Every day the Sun delivers 35,000 times more energy than the world requires.

Energy Facts
Americans use 15 times more energy than developing nations.

Do the Math

Changing from Incandescent to Fluorescent Bulbs

	Incandescent	Fluorescent
Brightness(lumens)	800	800
Power (watts)	60	15
Cost ($/kWh)	0.15	0.15
Lifetime (hours)	1000	9000
Price of bulb ($)	0.50	7.00
Price per year ($)	81	21.25
Price per year with bulbs ($)	85.50	28.25

$57.25 savings per year for changing from incandescent to fluorescent bulbs.

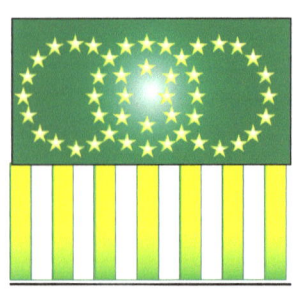

PV – Types

Monocrystaline	Polycrystaline	Thin Film (Amorphous)
13-16 % Efficient	10-13% Efficient	5-8% Efficient
35+ years	25+ years	20+ years
Requires less array area size Most expensive	Most common PV Moderate expense	Requires large array area

FAQ's (from the field)

Is there a difference between residential and commercial modules?

No, the difference between a residential and commercial installation is the amount of modules being used with the remaining equipment sized accordingly.

Will Solar PV work in my area?

Solar PV will work just about anywhere in the United States. Your installer will be able to inform you about just how much power you can receive at your location.

How much will a PV system cost for an 1800 ft^2 home?

PV systems are only concerned with how much electricity you are using, not how big your house or business is.

Can I heat my pool?

Theoretically the answer is yes, but there are much less expensive ways to achieve pool heating. See our section on Solar Pool Heating.

What effect does weather have on a PV system?

PV modules are weatherproof!

Will I be able to use my existing appliances with PV?

Absolutely yes.

How long will these PV modules last?

Most modules are warranted for at least 25 years (80% performance), and should last for at least 35 to 40 years.

How much roof space do I need?

With good orientation and no shading, 100 ft^2 of roof per kilowatt is a starting Rule of Thumb.

37	<u>Flexible</u>	37

Solar energy could handle any electrical or thermal load! Flexibility can expand the actual system, by changing from space heating in the winter to pool heat in the summer. Another example might be absorption-cooling for the summer, with space heating in the winter. How about pool heating in the summer, and driveway deicers for the winter?

Did You Know
That a Solar domestic hot water system replacing a natural gas hot water system will save over 10 tons of CO_2 emissions? If you are replacing an electric domestic hot water system, you'll be stopping over 70 tons of CO_2 from getting into the atmosphere.

Really!
World consumption of oil averages 84,979,000 barrels/day.

Energy Facts

<u>U.S. Electrical Generation Sources:</u>
Coal – 51%
Nuclear – 20%
Natural Gas – 18%
Oil – 2%
Renewable (hydropower dominating) – 9%

Do the Math
Traveling by train or bus is the least polluting to the atmosphere with only 0.22 lb CO_2 per mile traveled.

Solar Systems – Model House

Solar Pool Heating System
Pool Size - 30' X 15' X 5'
Specified 2 (20' x 10') Pool Collector Systems
With this system I am at 88% Collector ft^2 / Pool Area ft^2 which is on target for Long Island.

Solar Domestic Hot Water
Typical family of 4 usage approximately 80-100 gallons/day
Specified: Pre engineered, 2 Collector / 80 gallon storage, Solar DHW Package with everything
included to install the system, for the daily usage of 80 - 100 Gallons/Day.
This particular system has been calculated to save 75 - 78% of the DHW Load.

Solar PV System
Southern roof was capable of holding 450 ft^2 of PV panels.
Specified 27- (5' x 3') 185 Watt PV modules = 5 kW PV System.
This 5 kW system will offset customers usage by 6092 kWh /Year here on Long Island.
See Chart below to see what a 5 kW PV system will deliver in your city.

City	State	Facing South	Facing East	% difference of South	Facing West	% difference of South
NYC	New York	6092	4646	77	4570	75
LA	California	7349	5565	76	6096	83
Chicago	Illinois	5880	4515	77	4438	76
Houston	Texas	6099	5139	84	5229	86
Philadelphia	Pennsylvania	6030	4600	77	4559	76
Phoenix	Arizona	8085	6507	80	6405	80
San Diego	California	7492	5693	76	6264	83
Dallas	Texas	7017	5674	80	5764	82
San Jose	California	7230	5311	73	5840	80
Detroit	Michigan	5730	4449	77	4253	74
Indianapolis	Indiana	6119	4798	79	4728	77
Columbus	Ohio	5622	4465	79	4325	77
Baltimore	Maryland	6139	4652	76	4695	76
Memphis	Tennessee	6690	5359	80	5349	80
Seattle	Washington	4849	3413	70	3736	77
Portland	Oregon	5088	3646	71	4079	80
Boston	Massachusetts	6218	4664	75	4478	72
Denver	Colorado	7293	5744	79	5067	69

38	**Expandable**	38

All you need is the room to expand Solar power plants, wind farms, geothermal plants, and utility sized PV systems. In most cases, it is written in the initial plans of the project to expand in phases.

Did You Know

That PV modules will lose 0.5% efficiency for every degree Celsius increase in the temperature? PV modules work more efficiently in colder months. The additional summertime sunshine will compensate for higher output during the summer.

Really!

American electrical usage averages 10 to 12,000 kWh per year.
More in the summer, less in the winter.

Energy Facts

Top 10 Oil Reserve Countries (Billion Barrels)

Saudi Arabia	264
Iraq	113
United Arab Emirates	98
Kuwait	97
Iran	90
Venezuela	73
Russia	49
Libya	30
Mexico	28
China	24

No U.S.A.? Where do we stand with Iraq?

PV – Grid Tie

27 - 185W PV modules = 5 kW

Convenient equipment placement is outside, next to utility pole, utility meter with breaker box on inside wall.

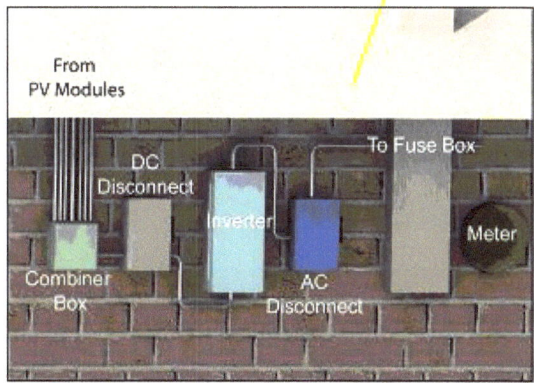

PV Panel - Sometimes called a module, the PV panel generates DC electricity directly from the Sun.

Combiner Box - Combines all of the PV panel wires into one box.

DC Disconnect - The switch to turn off the DC power for safety, servicing, or an emergency.

Inverter - Converts DC (direct current) power to AC (alternating current) power.

AC Disconnect - The switch to turn off the AC power for safety, servicing, or an emergency.

Breaker (fuse) Box is where your circuit breakers are located.

Utility Meter - The meter that keeps track of the electrical energy coming into and leaving the house.

Grid Tied PV System Operations

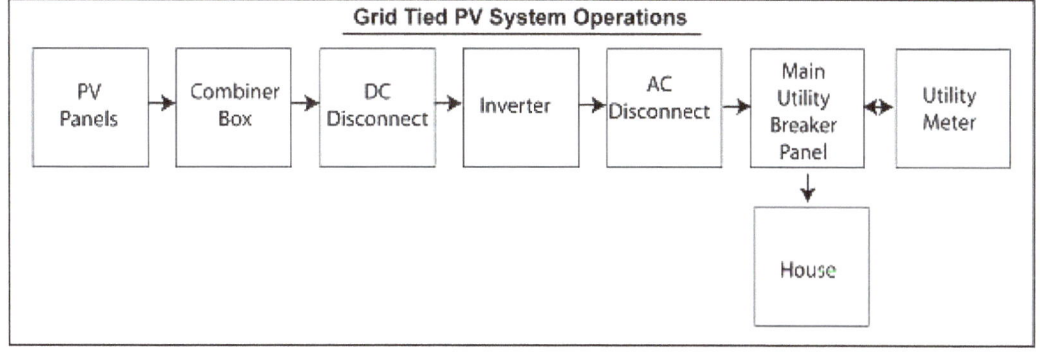

The Solar Advocate

Unless your system is under a PPA (Power Purchase Agreement), you'll never receive a bill for the amount of Sun that you use!

Did You Know

That if we can reduce our industrial energy demands by only 1%, we can save approximately 50,000,000 barrels of oil per year?

Really!

Palo Verde is the largest nuclear power plant in the United States with an output of 3,875 MW from their three reactors.

Energy Facts

In 2007 the United States electrical consumption was
3,923,000 814,000,000 kWh
servicing
142,121,652 customers.

Do the Math

10 hours of one 100 W incandescent light bulb equals seven hours of TV time.

 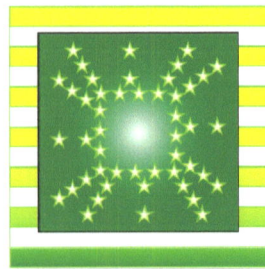 

PV – Off Grid

27 - 185 W PV modules = 5 kW

Convenient equipment placement is inside garage, next to breaker box, and on opposite side of wall to utility meter, and utility pole.

Batteries will need a well vented enclosed space.

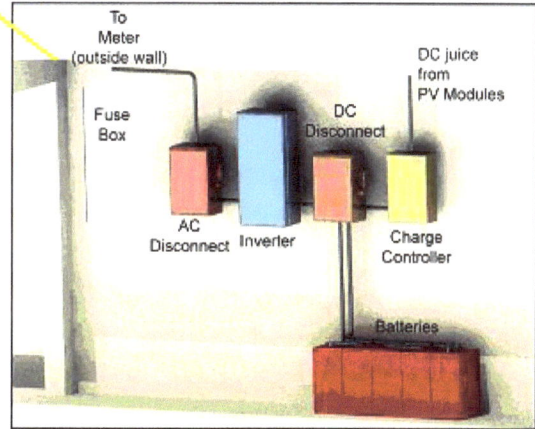

PV Panel - Sometimes called a module, the PV panel generates DC electricity directly from the Sun.

Charge Controller - Equipment responsible for charging the batteries with DC current.

DC Disconnect - The switch to turn off the DC power for safety, servicing, or an emergency.

Inverter - Converts DC (direct current) power to AC (alternating current) power.

AC Disconnect - The switch to turn off the AC power for safety, servicing, or an emergency.

Breaker (fuse) Box is where your circuit breakers are located.

Utility Meter - The meter that keeps track of the electrical energy coming into and leaving the house.

Batteries - Stores electricity in the form of DC power.

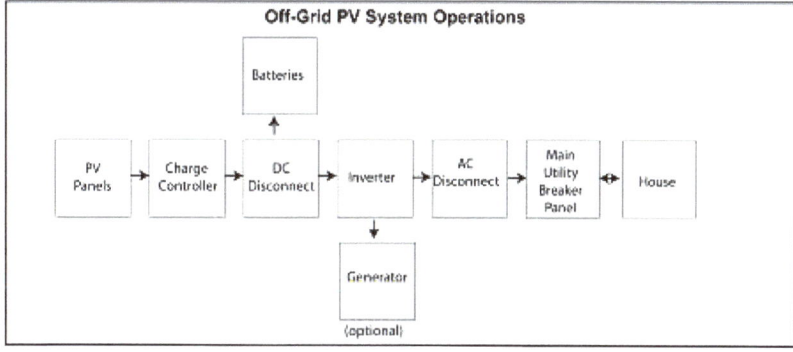

The Solar Advocate

A typical 500 MW coal plant, enough to power approximately 150,000 people, will burn 1.4 million tons of coal (40 train cars of coal per day) and will pollute 2.2 billion gallons of water each year.

Did You Know

That over 2 billion people around the world are without electricity?

Really!

In 1958 the Vanguard I was the first satellite that used Solar PV modules to generate electricity.

Energy Facts

There are 17,342 electrical utility generators in the United States.

Do the Math

PV will generate 17 jobs per million dollars.
Conventional energy will generate 4.73 jobs per million dollars.

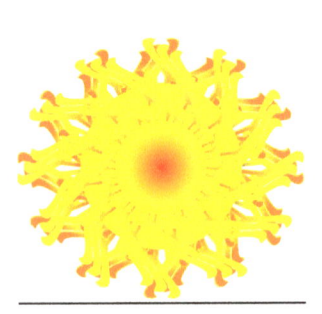 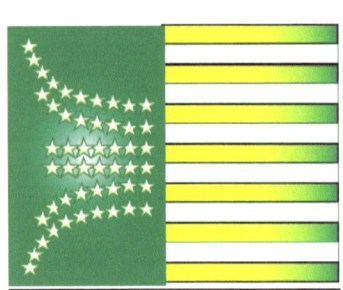 

Grid-Tied PV Versus Off-Grid PV

The grid refers to the national electric grid. Grid-tied, meaning that your PV Solar electric system will be connected to the national grid. When you're off-grid, the national electric grid is not connected to your system. The question is, do we go **grid-tied** or **off-grid**? The logical answer for properties that are currently on the grid is to stay on the grid and take advantage of net metering, if available. Knowing that you will always have a backup source of electricity is a good thought to have in the back of your head.

If your property is so rural that no wires or grid exists, and you cannot afford to have the utilities come out and place new transmission lines, then you will be forced to stay off the grid. If this is the situation, then I would consider going strictly DC, as you will probably get better performance out of your DC appliances. You realize you will have to buy all new DC appliances. No, you cannot interchange AC and DC appliances.

I had a client a few years back who insisted on going off the grid because of an argument he had with the utility company over pricing. He was angry that the transportation costs of the electricity he was using were more expensive than the electricity itself. A 5 kW off-grid system was installed, and my customer went off-line within 6 months of our initial meeting. Did I mention that he has since reconciled with the utility company after only two months of being off-grid? Divorce seemed to have been the subject of this decision.

41   Transportation Risks Reduced   41

The more Solar energy equipment in use, the less fossil fuel energy will be required to be transported. Remember, Solar energy gets delivered directly to your property. From the Sun directly to your roof, without interruption.

Did You Know
That renewable energy over the next 15 years can generate enough electricity to power 40 million homes, and that equates to 70 days of oil imports?

Really!
Energy saved from recycling one aluminum can will operate a TV or a computer for three hours. A six pack can save the energy of a car traveling 5 miles.

Energy Facts
In 2007, the United States' consumption of coal was 1,128 million tons which equals **2,256,000,000,000 lb**.

Do the Math

In Pennsylvania a 3 kW PV system will eliminate:
65 tons of CO_2 (global warming)
670 pounds of SO_2 (acid rain)
250 pounds of NO (smog),
YEARLY.

Net Metering

Net metering is the policy between the utility and its customer to receive their full share of credit when they supply the grid with green energy, whether it is from Solar PV or wind. Any excess electricity generated from your green energy system will go through your meter (have you ever seen your meter go backwards?) back into the grid where you will be given full credit for that energy. Think of it as a savings account, with the utility company holding on to your excess electricity, and when you require it, you can use it at any time. 42 states have already adopted some type of net metering policy. Part of your strategic planning of your PV or wind system will be getting the correct procedure for the interconnection of your system with your utility company. Some of the benefits of net metering might include: incentive to invest in clean energy, adaptability to small or large systems, enhances the competitiveness of alternative energy, and provides a fair and efficient way to utilize your alternative energy generated.

FAQ's (from the field):

Do I want to take advantage of net metering?
Yes.

Will I need to have my meter changed?
Yes. The utility will come out and change your meter to the digital type.

Am I eligible?
As of summer 2009:
No, if you live in Alaska, Tennessee, Alabama, or Mississippi.
Maybe, if you live in Idaho, Texas, or North Carolina (check your utility).
Yes, to everywhere else.

Will I still get electricity from the utility at night if I have a Solar PV system?
Yes, you will receive as much as you need. Have a party!

What happens during a power outage?
As long as there is no power coming from the utility, your PV System will not operate. The **safety** of the linesman is the reason for this. Could be quite challenging for the linesman to try to fix "live" wires.

What are the benefits of Net Metering?
The excess power that you have generated from your PV system will be valued at the full retail price.

42	**Reduced Power Plant Politics**	42

The new power plant for the 21st century is on your roof.

Did You Know
That 1 gallon of oil equals 150,000 BTU which equals 44.2 kWh?

Really!
An opened fireplace damper will send upward of 8 to 12% of your heating costs right up the chimney.

Energy Facts
Fuel costs:
Nuclear versus fossil fuel —
$0.5 per kilowatt hour versus $2.4 per kilowatt hour.

Do the Math
Flying today will put 0.638 lb CO_2 into the atmosphere for each mile traveled.

Shading Analysis Tools

PV hates shade! Your PV system's output can be greatly reduced by just a small amount of shade, and this is the reason why all potential PV sites should have some type of shade analysis, to verify that the system will work at its maximum potential.

PV Hates Shade! By placing a buisness card on a PV module, you can reduce your output by 27%!

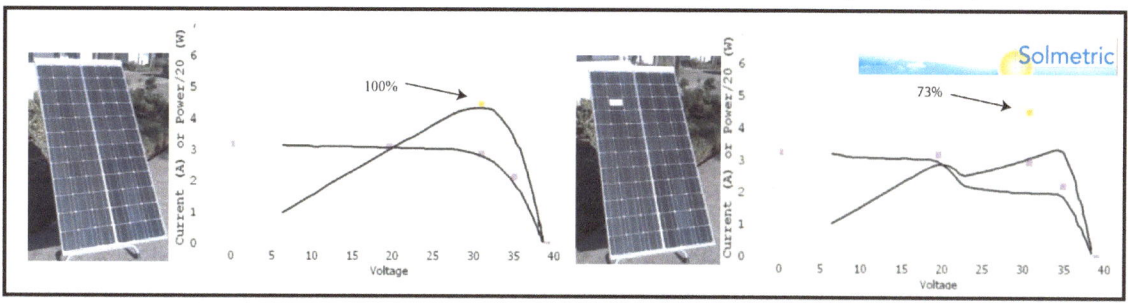

The Pathfinder is an instrument that will measure the Sun's potential for the entire year. It's non-electrical, so you do not have to look for external power, and is very easy to use. I have worked with Pathfinder for several years, and the results have saved me on numerous occasions. Recently, shade analysis is being requested by the utilities, to verify that the system will work as expected. It is recommended that if you have any type of obstructions (buildings or trees), you have a shade analysis done for the property. If it's trees we are concerned with, remember, they grow! With the expense of a PV system, I do not have any problem spending a little bit more for a shade analysis. It's a little insurance policy that is surely worthwhile. By the way, Pathfinder has competition from:

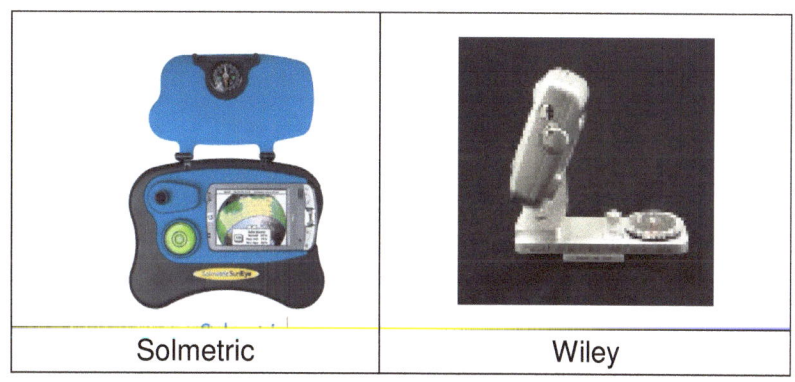

| Solmetric | Wiley |

| 43 | <u>Reflection of Your Personal Ethics</u> | 43 |

"If you are not part of the solution, you are part of the problem!"

  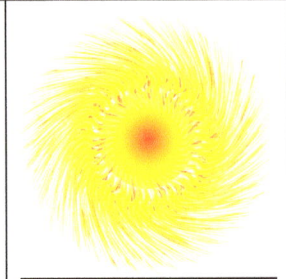

<u>Did You Know</u>

23% of carbon emissions worldwide, come from the United States?

<u>Really!</u>

75% of electricity used for electronics are used on phantom loads. This amount of electricity is equivalent to the output of 12 power plants.

<u>Energy Facts</u>

A business can save up to 90% of their electricity, space heating, and domestic hot water today with off-the-shelf items.

<u>Do the Math</u>   Carbon Emissions by Fuel

Fuel	lb CO_2	Unit
Oil	22.41	gallon
Natural gas	12.1	therm
LP	12.7	gallon
Kerosene	21.5	gallon
Gasoline	19.6	gallon
Coal	4,166	ton
Wood	3,814	ton

Phantom Loads

Phantom Loads — *(idle current, vampire power, wall wart)*

Phantom loads can be defined as that small amount of electricity that's being utilized by your electronic device when you think the power is off. An example of this is the clock on your oven, your VCR or DVD clock, and what about all of those lights on your computer that still remain on when you power off? 6% of our entire residential electrical consumption goes to phantom loads! This is excess electricity that we should try to reduce if not eliminate. Simply removing the plug from the outlet will reduce these phantom loads, and to the devices that you cannot shut down, for example your computer, there are devices that you can purchase to assist your reduction of this load.

	**Watt Stopper Plug Load Control** – pictured to the left is a smart power strip that will reduce these phantom loads. **MiniPower Minder** – pictured to the right, will shut off your computer's peripherals when you shut down. Every little bit helps!	

These are just a few of the devices that will reduce if not eliminate your phantom loads!

<u>What can I do?</u>
Unplug any device that is not in use.
Plug all of your devices into a power strip, and before you go to bed at night, turn it off.
Those large cube shaped transformers are 60% to 75% inefficient when plugged in, so either unplug it, or put into a power strip, and turn it off when not using.

44	**Abundance in Silicon**	44

Today's current technology of the PV utilizes silicon as the main ingredient, and did I mention that one of the most abundant substances in our Earth's crust is silicon? Silicon makes up 30% of the Earth's crust and is the 7th most common element in the Universe.

Did You Know
Oil, natural gas, and coal are being depleted at a rate 100,000 times faster than they were formed?

Really!
The annual 3021 KM Solar powered vehicle race in Australia, from Darwin to Adelaide:
1st year in 1987 average speed was 60 km/hr.
In 2005 the average speed was 103 km/hr.

Energy Facts
Solar roof shingles, Solar paint, and Solar nanotechnology will be the next generation in Solar energy.

Do the Math
Leading 9 PV States
California (530 MW), New Jersey (70.2 MW), Colorado (35.7 MW), Nevada (34.2 MW), Arizona (25.3 MW), New York (21.9 MW), Hawaii (15.8 MW), Connecticut (8.8 MW), Massachusetts (8.0 MW)
Great Solar PV activity in the northeast!

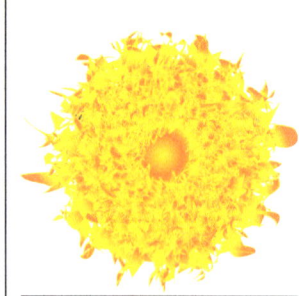

Sizing PV

When designing PV, the "design intent" is to have good Sun exposure between 9:00 A.M. and 3:00 P.M., hopefully with your roof facing southeast to southwest. I would like to, at this time, break it up into commercial and residential:

Residential – once you have completed your site analysis and have decided which roof or roofs will be used for your PV system, and this includes a shading analysis if required, the maximum available area of roof will be calculated. This area will then be divided by the square footage of the module, to give us the maximum PV system size available. This is a starting point. At this time, if I know the customer's electric load (from his monthly bill), I will be able to calculate an approximate Solar fraction (Solar PV contribution/homes total load.) At this time, it would be up to the customer to decide final size. This is where the installer and the customer will talk economics.

Commercial – most commercial applications are on flat roofs, which make sizing a lot more versatile. Once again as in residential, we are trying to calculate the maximum available roof space for our PV system. Remember, PV hates shading! Stay away from all mechanical equipment on the roof, as we're looking to maximize output. By knowing the area and the square footage of our module, we can calculate the maximum PV size. To maximize the project size, installers will calculate the modules being flat on the roof. I highly recommend at least a 7° tilt for rain runoff, which will remove more of the dirt off the modules, then if flat. Dirty modules reduce performance.

Now, it is time to talk to the owner about your recommendations on size (in which economics will play an important role), equipment type, type of mounting hardware, estimated installation times and schedules. From my experience, for commercial PV projects, you will need an electrical engineer to sign off on any electrical diagrams submitted to the utility company, and a structural engineer to do any kind of load analysis work on the roof due to the excess weight from the system itself.

Prepackaged PV Systems

Over the past year or so, more PV suppliers have put together pre-engineered systems to assist you. These packages will have all the components from mounting hardware, inverters, modules, wiring diagrams, to all of the nuts and bolts. I recommend these systems because they normally carry a small discount, and everything I need for an easy installation will be at the job site, normally delivered at the same time.

The Solar Advocate

Net metering will enable PV and wind users to sell back to the utility the unused power that is generated from their system. You will be credited for all of the PV generated electricity you put into the grid, and will be reimbursed accordingly. Please check your local utility for more information.

Did You Know

There are more than 20,000 Solar powered water pumping stations in operation worldwide?

Really!

The Sun's average surface temperature is 5700 ℃.
The Earth's average surface temperature is 20 ℃.

Energy Facts

Refrigerators in the United States use the equivalent of sixty 300 MW power plants.
If we were to switch to Energy Star products, we could potentially cut that in half to thirty 300 megawatt power plants.

Do the Math

A 1 kW PV system will save each month:
170 lb of coal
350 lb of CO_2
105 gal of water

Metering/Monitoring

Every Solar system should have some type of meter and or monitor, in order to check its performance. Recently, in California, the CPUC has required that all residential and commercial customers install a monitor to record output. Some of the benefits of monitoring:

- Instant visibility of system performance
- Anticipate any operating problems
- Maximize energy output
- Increase financial performance
- Up-to-the-minute reports
- Public awareness
- Web based – anywhere, anytime reporting

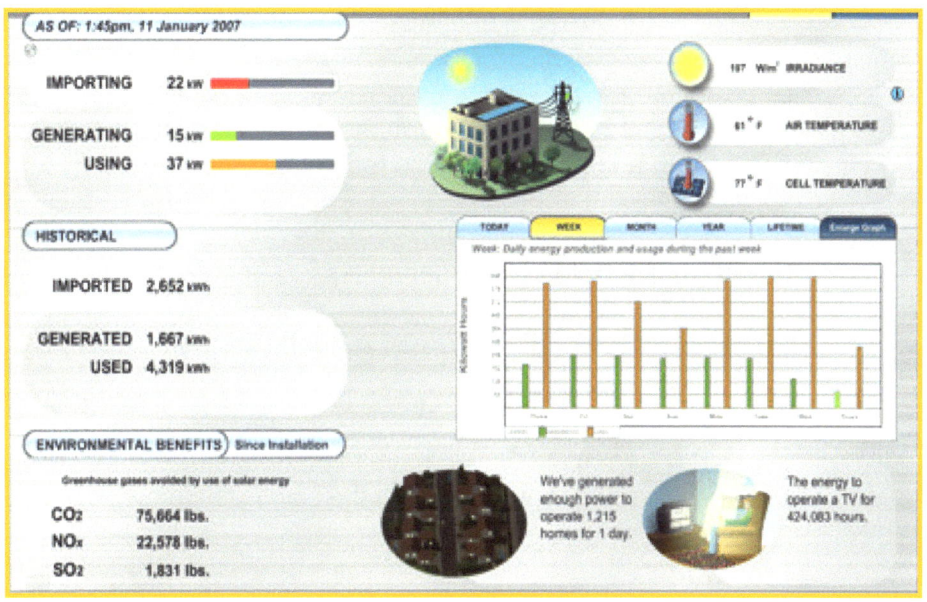

The above diagram shows the output of a PV system, courtesy of Fat Spaniel. Fat Spaniel has a full line of metering and monitoring equipment for your PV system. They can be reached at http://www.fatspaniel.com for more information.

The Solar Advocate

The Sun strikes a thermal collector and it generates heat.
The Sun strikes a PV module and it generates electricity.
The wind strikes a wind turbine and it generates electricity.
Just that simple!

Did You Know

In Tokyo, Japan, there are over 1.5 million Solar domestic hot water systems, and that's more than in the entire United States?

Really!

Did you know that a refrigerator from the 80s uses almost twice as much electricity as a new Energy Star product? The best part about Energy Star rated products is that you potentially will get a tax credit from the federal government.

Energy Facts

Grand Coulee (Hydroplant) generates 7,079 MW of power

= 7.079 GW (gigawatts).

Do the Math

100,000,000,000 tons of TNT (dynamite) would have to be detonated every second to compare energy output with the Sun.

Balance of System (BOS)

Balance of system (BOS) is the term used for all of the activities and equipment used in a PV system, other than the actual PV module.

What's behind the installation of a PV system:

- Sales call
- Site visit
- Permitting
- Layout of the modules
- The selection and purchase of the inverters
- The design, selection and purchase of mounting hardware
- The design, selection and purchase of disconnects
- Wiring diagrams
- Start up and testing
- Electrical interconnection
- The design, selection, and purchase of metering and monitoring equipment
- Financing
- Operation and maintenance
- Protection and safety

Installation of a PV system is a project, and with a proper, experienced installer, this journey to going green should be smooth sailing.

FAQ's (from the field)

Who pulls the permit?
The PV installer should be filling out all of the permits, and applying for them. Your signature will probably be required.

What is the estimated time of installation?
Depending on the size, a typical residential job (less than 10 kW) could take several months to have installed. This is from the initial sales visit to the actual operation of the system The actual equipment installation will take only a few days; it's the permitting, designing, and electrical interconnection that will take up most of the time.

On the commercial side, a properly installed system will take months before the system is online. The requirements to put up a commercial system are a little bit more involved than a residential system. Sit back and relax, because when your system is up and running , and you're watching your meter go backwards, it will all be worth the wait.

| 47 | Great Educational Tool | 47 |

It's a fun way to learn about energy. All systems will be outside, and did I mention class trips?

Did You Know
That an average American family will use approximately 12 barrels of oil per household per year?

Really!
One drop of water per second leaking from your faucet could total 175 gallons per month, and if that's hot water, money down the drain? Around $70 per year can be lost if you don't fix your leaky faucets.

Energy Facts
617 facilities burning coal to generate electricity in the United States,
476 power plants selling electricity as the main business and
141 industrial, commercial institutions generating electricity on location.

A Bit of History
Did you know Archimedes defended Syracuse by attacking the Roman fleet with Solar reflectors (polished brass) and setting their sails on fire, in turn, burning down the ships?

PV Economics

As of the summer of 2009, the prices for PV systems installed are holding steady between:

7.50 – 9.00 $/W

PV modules are being priced at 3.50-4.25 $/W

Typical Installed PV System Prices	
1 kW	$7500-$9000
3 kW	$22,500-$27,000
5 kW	$37,500-$45,000
7 kW	$52,500-$63,000
10 kW	$75,000-$90,000
These prices do not include any federal, state or utility rebates or incentives.	

Before you sign the PV contract:
- Get more then one bid, and let these installers know that you are 'shopping.'
- Stick with standard (off-the-shelf) mounting systems.
- Stick with a pre-engineered, packaged PV system.
- Avoid customizing.

Check your state and local utility for any Solar incentives! It could make the difference!

5 KW System @ 8 $/W Output will be approx 500 kWh/Month			
	Long Island (LIPA-3.5 $/W)	New York (NYSERDA 3 $/W)	CT (CE 5 $/W)
Cost	$40,000	$40,000	$40,000
Utility rebate	$17,500	$15,000	$25,000
Net	$22,500	$25,000	$15,000
State	$5,000	$5,000	-
Federal	$6,750	$7,500	$4,500
Net	$10,750	$12,500	$10,500
Payback	9 years	10 years	9 years

These prices do not reflect any increased price in electricity.

48	Portability	48

With the ability of Solar PV cells to be made in any size or shape, the portability factor of Solar is here. As long as there is Sun, anywhere on Earth, you can generate electricity! With electricity, you could run anything!

Did You Know
That 208,000 homes in the United States are using some type of PV for their electrical needs?

Really!
Sunlight to electricity is 10 times more efficient than photosynthesis.

Energy Facts
In 2006 the renewable energy industry in the United States did approximately $40 billion in revenue, and created 194,000 jobs.

Do the Math
In 2007, renewable sources (mostly hydro-power) accounted for 7% of the total U.S. energy consumption, which equaled 9.4% electrical generation.

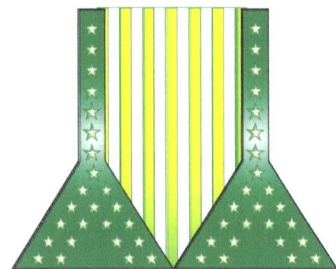

Solar Lighting

Solar lighting has been making more of an impact recently with the price of fuel going up the way it has. A typical Solar lighting system will gather energy during the day, store it in a battery, and when the light is required at night, with the use of LEDs, your area is now lit up.

Applications for **Solar lighting** may include:
- Parking lots
- Driveways
- Bus shelters
- Parks
- Docks and piers
- Sidewalks and paths
- Campuses
- Billboards and signs
- Streets and roadways
- Remote operations/temporary sites
- Gardens

Components of Solar Lighting
- Solar Cell - converts sunlight to electricity
- Battery - (rechargeable) stores energy
- Light Emitting Diode - provides light
- Photo Resistor - detects presence of light
- Control Circuit - the brains
- External Casing - protection

Why Solar Lighting?
- Minimal operation cost
- Low purchase price
- No licensed electrician required (in most cases)
- No trenching (unless there is a backup)
- Saves energy
- Easy installation

| 49 | Reduce Your Energy Bill | 49 |

The first month your system goes online, you save money. The size of the system will determine how much money you will be saving.

Did You Know
Solar thermal power plants will create 2-1/2 times as many skilled high-paying jobs as conventional power plants do?

Really!
New commercial fluorescent lighting systems use less than half the energy as compared to the 1980s.

Energy Facts
Solar energy can be transformed into chemical energy (photosynthesis), electrical energy (PV), heat energy (flat-plate collector), and mechanical energy (windmills and Stirling engines).

Do the Math
France went from 0% to 79% nuclear in less than 20 years.

Solar Computer Design

The computer programs that have assisted me in designing Solar energy systems are as follows:

T-Sol – Solar Thermal planning and design, including pool heat. Can be reached at http://www.solar-software.com

PV-Sol – Solar PV planning and design, from the same company as T-Sol. Can be reached at http://www.solar-software.com

F. Chart – Solar thermal planning and design. I used F. Chart from 1978 to 1981, and always received good results. Back in 1980 I was using a phone modem for access.

RET Screen – good online program for both PV and thermal. Go to http://www.retscreen.net for a free download.

PV Watts – simple online program for PV. The PV calculations in this book came from PV Watts. Go to http://www.NREL.org

Sol – Sim – very simple and easy to use, for Solar domestic hot water systems.

Pathfinder – once you gather your information from the instrument, you can plug it into the program and get some good performance analysis.

I realize that there are probably a lot more computer programs to be used for Solar energy, I just don't have the time to work with all of them. I have been a fan of **T-Sol** for a few years now. Very easy to use, available with English units, and it prints out good reports.

P.S. I will look at any program that will make my occupation more efficient and easier.

The Solar Advocate

Solar equipment properly designed, installed, and maintained will last for years! Most thermal collectors have warrantees for 10 years, and most PV modules guarantee 80% performance after 25 years. What else do you have in your house that will carry these warrantees?

Did You Know

That Solar energy demand has grown an average of 25% yearly over the last 15 years, and is still growing?

Really!

In 2008, federal buildings used 20% less energy per square foot than in 1984.

Energy Facts

In 2007, the U.S. consumption of coal was 1,128,000,000 tons with 81,278 miners.

Do the Math

Highest electrical rate in the United States – Hawaii – 0.2129 $/kWh.
Lowest electrical rate in the United States – Idaho – 0.05 $/kWh.
These prices do not cover taxes or transportation costs!

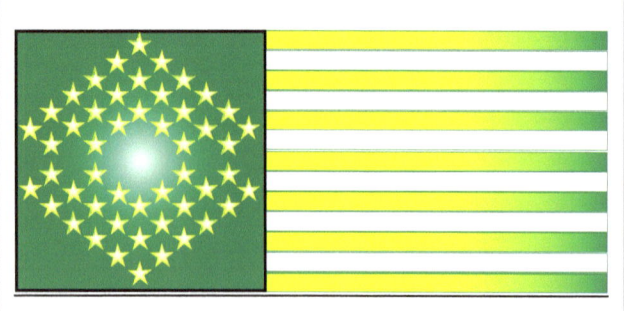

Selecting a Contractor

Installing a Solar system, whether it is PV or thermal, will be one of the biggest investments of your life. You're looking for the best job at a reasonable cost. From my experience, I have found that installers who have actual pictures of their past experience will do better than the novice who has no experience.

Things to keep in mind when selecting a contractor:

- Speak to at least 4 installers to compare system features, warrantees, costs, and expected annual output for your project. When comparing contractors' proposals, do not mix apples with oranges. Compare a 10 kW system from one company to another 10 kW system from another.
- It is not necessary for the salesman to come to the house for the first visit. With the combination of Google Earth, the company's website, a phone, and a good salesman, you should be able to get a quote either by e-mail or by snail mail. If you like what you see, then invite them over to the house for a site visit.
- It's mandatory to see pictures of their existing and working projects. This will be the work that they do on your property!
- I would not deal with anyone who has no experience, no license, or no training.
- Get references, and actually call them!
- Is the contractor insured and fully licensed?
- Does the installer have a clean legal history?
- Get everything in writing.
- Is the company financially stable?
- Will the installer be in charge of permitting?
- Does the installer know all of the rebates and incentives for the local area?
- Do they have financing options, and what about payment terms?
- How long have they been installing systems?
- What's the approximate install time?
- Are they using subcontractors?
- Do you understand the contract?
- Are you comfortable with this installer in your house and on your roof?

51	Versatile	51

Solar energy can be used to generate electricity, generate heat, cook, dry clothes and run water pumps, to name just a few uses of the Sun's versatility. Anything that requires power can be run by the Sun.

Did You Know

A megawatt (MW) = 1,000,000 watts?
1 GW = 1000 MW.
Most power plants fall in the several megawatt range, with a few in the gigawatts.

Really!

There are over 250,000 Solar pool heating systems in the United States.

Energy Facts

There are 104 nuclear reactors in the United States. Illinois and Pennsylvania have the most reactors, with six and five respectively.

Do the Math

1 ton of sand (silicon) will generate an equivalent to 500,000 **tons** of coal.
At 40,000 pounds/truck, 25,000 trucks would be required, and that would stretch 189 miles long.

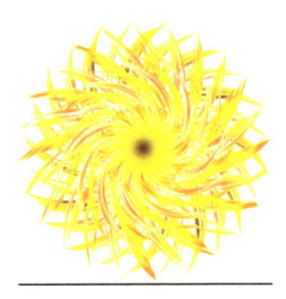  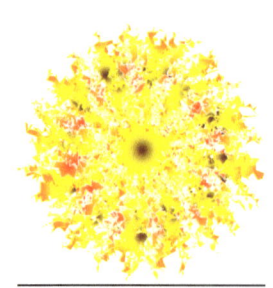

Financing Solar

Because of the cost of Solar energy systems, financing is a growing option. If financing is the option, please take into account of all of the federal and state tax incentives and rebates. Remember, a rebate is money that you will get back, and a tax credit will be applied to your income tax when you apply for your federal taxes. A few ideas about financing Solar:

Installer Financing – the more experienced the Solar installer, the chances are that he will be working with financial institutions to finance the system(s) that he will be installing on your roof. Installer should inform you of any available financing from him.

Bank – I would talk to my personal banker second, and find out if there are any "green" loans available. Recently, banking institutions have been introducing the "green" loan, with very low interest rates.

Credit cards – I personally would hesitate to use a credit card to finance my Solar system because of the interest rate being way too high. I would use my credit card to get the points and pay off the charge, hopefully with the next statement. Be careful of the credit card interest rates! Be careful of credit cards.

Power Purchase Agreements (PPA) – is an arrangement between a third-party investor and property owner, where a homeowner will purchase discounted energy from the investor's system that is installed on your roof. I recommend an attorney look at this agreement before you sign, as all are a little bit different.

Leasing – as more and more financial institutions are getting into the green movement, leasing is gaining momentum among commercial applications. Consult your accountant.

Grant Programs – check your state and local governments for any type of grants available for alternative energy. The feds also have some pretty good grant programs that can be found online.

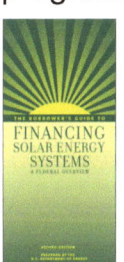

The Borrower Guide to Financing
Solar Energy Systems: a Federal Overview
A good PDF with government-sponsored financing packages, with names and phone numbers to get the ball rolling. This PDF can be found online at the Department of Energy. Worth a look!

The Solar Advocate

No oil tanker hijacking, no kidnapping, no loose nukes, no oil embargoes, no shortages, no traveling to enemy territories, and no politics.

Did You Know

That the United States imports over 20 million barrels of oil a day?

Really!

Over half the world's PV supply goes to Japan and Germany.

Energy Facts

The Sun's energy is carried by photons to Earth.

Do the Math

Food travels an average of more than 1,000 miles, requiring 10 times the petroleum energy to produce than its Solar food value (calorie). Are we eating oil?

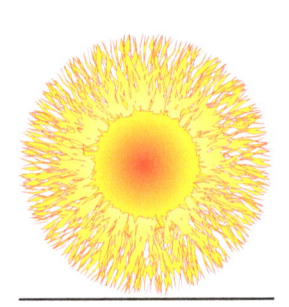  

Tax Incentives

The federal government is behind alternative energy, to the point where they are willing to assist your financing with a tax credit for your "green" system. I mention tax credit because if you're not paying taxes to the federal government, there are no incentives. The federal incentives are tax credits and not rebates. Rebates will send you the actual funds, and you're more likely to get a rebate check from a utility than the federal or state government.

Federal Incentives for Renewable Energy:
For residential, commercial, and industrial:
PV – 30% tax credit with no cap
Thermal – 30% tax credit with no cap
Wind – 30% tax credit with no cap

State Incentives For Renewable Energy:
For updated state incentives go online to http://www.dsireusa.org for a full listing of each state with respect to tax incentives for purchasing renewable energy.

Check with your local authorities and utilities to see if your local town is offering any kind of rebates or tax incentive.

State	PV Incentive	Thermal Incentive	No Sales Tax	No Property Tax Increase	Personal Tax	Corporate Tax
New York	Y	Y	Y	Y	Y	Y
California	Y	Y	N	Y	N	N
Illinois	Y	Y	Y	Y	N	N
Texas	Y	Y	N	Y	N	Y
Pennsylvania	Y	Y	N	Y	Y	Y
Arizona	Y	Y	Y	Y	Y	Y
Michigan	Y	Y	N	Y	N	N
Indiana	N	N	N	Y	N	N
Ohio	N	Y	Y	Y	N	N
Maryland	Y	Y	Y	Y	Y	Y
Tennessee	N	N	N	Y	N	N
Washington	Y	Y	Y	N	N	N
Oregon	Y	Y	N	Y	Y	Y
Massachusetts	Y	Y	Y	Y	Y	Y
Colorado	Y	Y	Y	Y	N	N
New Jersey	Y	Y	Y	Y	N	N
Florida	Y	Y	Y	Y	Y	N
As of summer 2009 - check for any updates.						

53	No Acid Rain	53

Solar systems do not have chimneys.

Did You Know
1 kW Solar energy PV system equals the burning of 170 pounds of coal, with approximately 350 pounds of carbon dioxide being released into the atmosphere per month?

Really!
Air pollutants (NO & SO_2) harm humans.
Greenhouse gases (CO_2) harm the Earth and affect climate change.

Energy Facts

250 million cars in the U.S.A. should be thinking about saving energy:
Do the speed limit (between 30 – 65 is the sweet spot).
Keep tire inflation correct.
No idling (0 mpg).
Drive sensible (aggressive driving and braking will reduce MPG consumption by 33%).
Walk or ride a bicycle if you can.
Reduce the weight (100 extra pounds will reduce mpg 12 percent).
A reminder: 20 pounds of carbon dioxide for each gallon of gasoline burned!

Gadgets

How many batteries do you go through in a year?

Tote bag	Air purifier	Calculator
Dress	Car ventilator	Clock
Cool hat	Flashlight	Refrigerator/cooler
House numbers	Decorative lights	Parasol

The Solar Advocate

54	No Greenhouse Gases	54

Solar energy systems do not have chimneys.

Did You Know

That every second, 4,000,000 tons of hydrogen are consumed by the Sun?

Really!

It takes 90% less energy to recycle an aluminum can than to make a new one.

Energy Facts

Solar PV modules work more efficiently in the winter than in summer.

Do the Math

Wind farms in the United States kept over 16,000,000 pounds of pollutants from entering our atmosphere in 2008.

 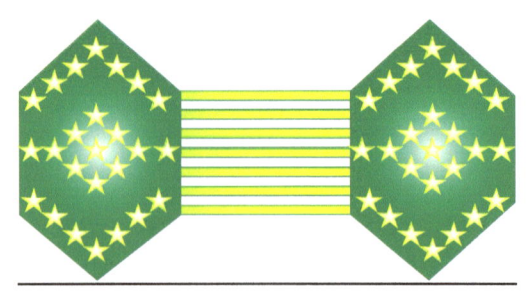 

Gadgets

Radio	Pocketbook	Recharger
Rodent killer	Robots	Shower
Visor	Recharging sunglasses	USB charger
Weatherproof speakers	Bikini	Windmill

55	New Industries Are Being Formed	55

New companies are being formed every day with the American entrepreneurial spirit. I have met a lot of people that are banking on the Solar industry over the next 10 to 20 years.

Did You Know
357 MW of electricity were produced by PV in the United States in 2008?

Really!
Laptops use 90% less energy than a desktop.

Energy Facts
There are 452,768 natural gas wells in the United States, connected by 301,965 miles of pipeline.

Do the Math
PV systems are completely automatic and are suitable for unmanned operations.

Energy Star

http://www.energystar.gov

Founded in 1992, Energy Star is a joint program of the United States EPA and the United States DOE, helping us save money and protect the environment through energy-efficient products and practices. In 2007, Energy Star was responsible for reducing greenhouse gas emissions equivalent to 27 million cars. The agency has various programs that will save the residential and commercial energy user. Energy Star qualifies energy products in more than 50 categories, and each one of these products must meet a strict energy-efficiency criteria. Appliances, heating and cooling equipment, water heaters, home electronics, home envelope products, office equipment, lighting equipment, and commercial food services are among some of the categories that any tea stall will qualify. For more information, go to http://www.energystar.gov, and I am sure that you will be on your way to energy savings. Energy Star does not have any specific Solar savings, rebates, or incentive programs, but the backup equipment that is used with Solar should have an Energy Star rating, and you can receive an additional rebate for these backup systems with guaranteed good energy-efficiency. Take advantage of the good work that Energy Star is doing for this country.

The Solar Advocate

The more PV that is being used, the less energy will be required from the power plants, which will decrease power output, which will ease up the grid, adding years of life back to grid.

Did You Know

That 6.8 GW of PV were produced in 2008 worldwide?

Really!

Total number of phantom loads (idle TV, VCR, DVD, stove light, clocks, computers) can equate to 2 million cars worth of pollution each year.

Energy Facts

The largest oil refinery in the United States is in Baytown, Texas, putting out 567,000 barrels per day, and is owned by Exxon.

Do the Math

National average emissions for electricity is 1.64 pounds of CO_2 per kilowatt hour.
Average American household averages 1000 kWh per month = 19,680 pounds CO_2 per year per household.

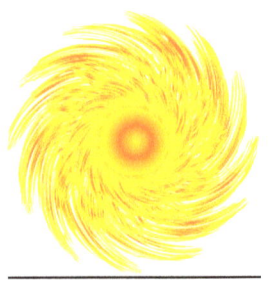 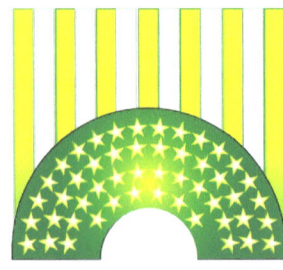 

Saving Energy

If you are considering a Solar energy system, you have energy savings on your mind. Here are some additional tips to save you energy, and help your Solar energy system work that much more efficiently:

- Space heaters can be used to heat the room that you're in, versus heating the whole house.
- Use ceiling fans instead of air-conditioners
- Change incandescent light bulbs to compact fluorescent.
- Replace your 1980 appliances with new Energy Star qualified products.
- Attic fans (whole house fans) can substantially reduce air conditioning.
- Wash clothes in cold water.
- Insulate and weatherproof.
- Do you have a programmable thermostat?
- Instantaneous hot water system over conventional hot water tank.

I Googled "saving energy" and received 94,800,000 available websites!

Additional Saving Energy Tips:
- Unplug any unused appliances.
- Your charger should not be left in the wall after you are finished recharging your phone.
- Turn your hot water tank thermostat down to 120°.
- Use full loads in the dishwasher and washing machine.
- Install low-flow showerheads.
- Clean your dryer's lint filter.
- Check that your refrigerator is completely sealed (if it doesn't hold a dollar bill, it's time for a new refrigerator).
- Repair leaky faucets.
- Replace your air filters.
- Are all of your water pipes insulated?
- In the winter, let the Sun shine in; in the summer, shade the Sun.

57 | Transmission/Distribution Lines Will Be Reduced | 57

The more local the power plants (PV on your roof) the less transmission lines will be required.

Did You Know
That the Sun is 93,000,000 miles away, and it takes only eight minutes for a photon of light to travel to Earth?

Really!
In one second, the Sun releases more energy then mankind has consumed since the Big Bang!

Energy Facts

Price of oil can be broken down as follows:	
Marketing	46%
Crude	42%
Refining	12%

Do the Math
Texas has the largest number of refineries in the United States, converting some 4,509,196 barrels a day.

The Solar Advocate

58	Less Coal to Be Mined	58

Coal is the leading fuel to generate electricity in the United States. More PV systems, less coal required means less mining.

Did You Know
That Solar energy is the oldest form of energy, being around for around 4.5 billion years?

Really!
83% of the United States' air pollution comes from the production of electricity.

International Energy Agency defining **Renewable Energy**
"Renewable Energy is derived from natural processes that are replenished constantly. In its various forms, it derives directly from the Sun, or from heat generated deep within the Earth. Included in the definition is electricity and heat generated from Solar, wind, ocean, hydropower, biomass, geothermal resources, biofuels, and hydrogen derived from renewable resources."

A Bit of History
In 1871, American Charles Wilson built a Solar still at a Chilean copper mine, and was producing 4,000 gallons a day of fresh water from saltwater.

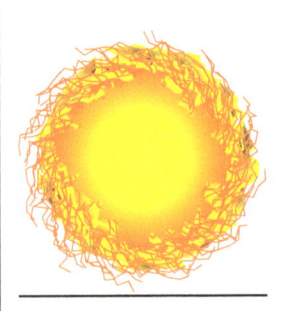  

Renewable Energy

HydroPower

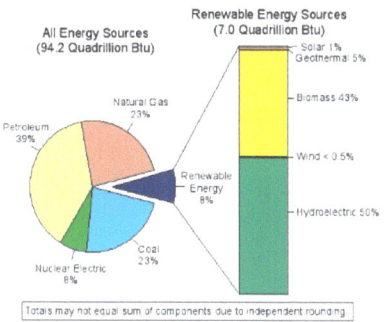

Hoover Dam

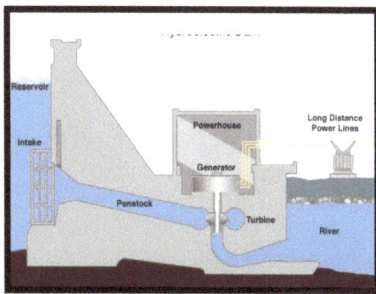

How they work

Americas Largest

Grand Coulee Dam

Capacities of some large dams:

Grand Coulee	1942	6500 MW
John Day	1969	2200 MW
Niagara (NY)	1961	2000 MW
The Dalles	1957	1800 MW
Chief Joseph	1956	1500 MW
McNary	1954	1400 MW
Hoover	1936	1345 MW
Glen Canyon	1964	950 MW
Three Gorges	2005	18000 Mw

Tidal Power is coming soon
to an Ocean near you!

And they work at night

59	Reduction of Nuclear Power	59

Replacing nuclear power plants with PV farms? Not probable, but it's a nice thought. One day!

Did You Know

That Solar energy systems have been supplying power to all of our satellites since the 50s? This was the beginning of the PV industry.

Really!

In six hours, deserts receive more energy from the Sun than mankind uses in one year.

Energy Facts

Solar photovoltaic devices are dependent on light, not heat.

Do the Math

Sources of CO_2 Emissions

Vehicles	51%
Appliances	26%
Heating and cooling	18%
Waste	5%

Renewable Energy

Geothermal Energy

From the Heat in the Earth

Temperatures in the Earth

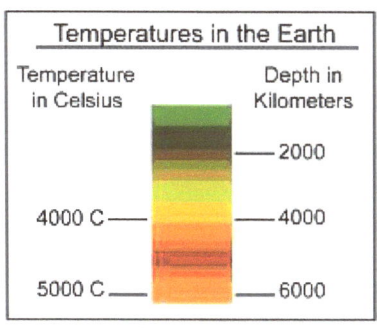

Temperature in Celsius

Depth in Kilometers

— 2000

4000 C — — 4000

5000 C — — 6000

Why Geothermal Works

Geothermal Resources

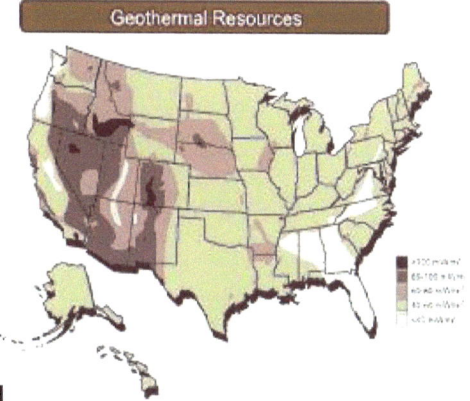

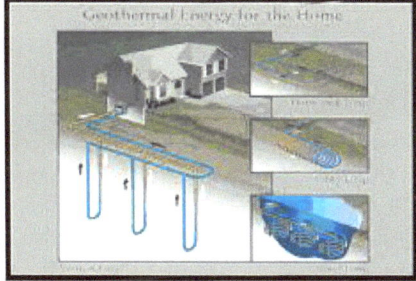

Residential

Industrial

Geothermal Power Plants
Do not emit any CO_2,
or pollutants,
just Water Vapor!

Commercial

The Solar Advocate

60	Reduces CO$_2$ Emissions	60

Like I've said, Solar energy products have no chimneys.

 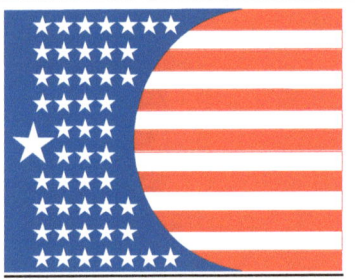 

Did You Know
100 mi^2 of PV in the southwest of the United States has the potential to supply all of the electrical needs for the entire country?

Really!
The U.S. receives more Solar energy in 40 minutes than we use in fossil fuel for the entire year.

Energy Facts

How do you say Solar in:
Spanish – solar
French – solaire
Italian – solare
Dutch – zone

Do the Math
The average lifetime energy consumption of one person in the United States is approximately 170 tons of coal, 2000 barrels of oil, and 7.5 MCF of natural gas,
x 306,000,000 Americans.
WOW!

 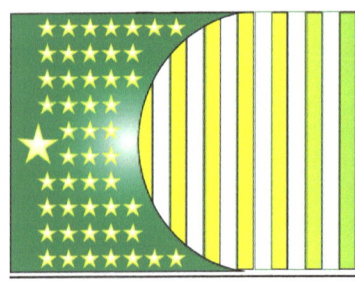 

132

Renewable Energy

Wind Energy

Residential

Commercial

Agriculture

National Total Power Capacities (MW)

Existing	Under Construction
29,440 MW	5,866 MW

State Total Power Capacities (MW)

Top 10

State	Existing	Under Construction
Texas	8,361	1,096
Iowa	3,043	409
California	2,787	20
Minnesota	1,805	40
Washington	1,575	405
Oregon	1,408	426
New York	1,264	21
Colorado	1,068	174
Kansas	1,014	0
Illinois	915	703

Ocean Wind Farm

Wind Farms

I'm Thinking Colorado

A Future Style?

Turbines Work at Night

61	Reduce Global Warming	61

Reduce your carbon footprint with Solar, and you will reduce global warming.

Did You Know
That concentrating Solar collectors generate steam, which will turn a turbine to generate electricity?

Really!
Solar energy is technically feasible, economically sound, and environmentally attractive.

Energy Facts

United States' 10 Sunniest Cities

Yuma	90%	Flagstaff	79%
Las Vegas	85%	Fresno	79%
Phoenix	85%	Reno	79%
Tucson	85%	Sacramento	78%
El Paso	83%	Albuquerque	76%

A Bit of History
In 1878, August Mouchot demonstrated a Solar cooker at the World Exhibition in Paris.

Associations/Organizations

Solar Energy Industry Association
http://www.seia.org/cs/governmen

American Solar Energy Society
http://www.ases.org/

Arizona Solar Energy Association
http://www.azSolarcenter.com/index.html

BASEA – Boston Area Solar Energy
Association
http://www.basea.org/

Colorado Renewable Energy Society
http://www.cres-energy.org/index.html

El Paso Solar Energy Association
http://www.epsea.org

Florida Renewable Energy Association
http://www.cleanenergyflorida.org/index.html

Great Lakes Renewable Energy Association
http://www.glrea.org/

Illinois Renewable Energy Association
http://www.illinoisrenew.org/

Iowa Renewable Energy Association
http://www.irenew.org/workshops.html

Maine Solar Energy Association
http://www.maineSolar.org/

The Mid Atlantic Renewable Energy
Association
http://www.paenergyfest.com/

Midwest Renewable Energy
Association
http://www.the-mrea.org/

Minnesota Renewable Energy
Society
http://www.mnrenewables.org/

New Mexico Solar Energy
Association
http://nmsea.org/index.php

NESEA – North East Sustainable
Energy Association
http://www.nesea.org/

Northern California Solar Energy
Association
http://www.norcalSolar.org/

North Carolina Solar Center
http://www.ncsc.ncsu.edu/

Pocono Northeast Solutions
http://www.pnesolutions.org/

Potomac Region Solar Energy
Association
http://www.prsea.org/

San Luis Valley Solar Association
http://www.slv-Solar.org/index.htm

Solar Oregon
http://www.Solaroregon.org/

Texas Solar Energy Society
http://txses.org/index.php

62 — Watch Your Meter Go Backwards — 62

Have you ever seen your electric meter go backwards? There always seems to be a smile on the customer's face when they're watching their meter go backwards.

Did You Know
That Einstein won the Nobel peace prize for his work on photoelectrics, and not the Special Law of Relativity? Thanks Al!

Really!
It is estimated that 16,000,000 tons of CO_2 is created by the world on a daily basis.

Energy Facts
Hydropower is the fourth largest supplier of electricity in the United States.

Do the math
As soon as a Solar system, whether it's PV or thermal, is installed, you will immediately start saving energy and money.

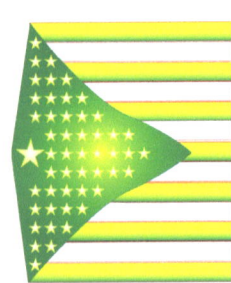

Solar Myths

Solar is ugly

Beauty is in the eyes of the beholder. I highly recommend that while you're in the initial stages of purchasing Solar, you look at pictures of existing jobs that the installer has already done. This will be the indication of what your system will look like when installed.

Solar is expensive

Solar energy systems are an investment, and are expensive. With the federal tax credit and state incentives, along with some utility rebates, Solar energy systems are now in the market to be affordable.

Solar is a poor investment

Solar energy systems have a lifetime of over 30 years, with a ROI (return on investment) of over 15%. Solar is a good investment.

Solar only works in warm climates

Solar energy systems work anywhere the Sun shines! PV performance actually decreases in warmer climates. I agree Solar thermal works better in San Diego then Portland, Maine in the winter, but I'm still saving 50% of my domestic hot water load.

Solar cannot serve any significant fraction of the U.S. electrical needs

A 10 x 10 mile PV array can serve the entire United States with electricity. I recommend we put 2 square miles of PV in each state.

PV cannot offset Environmental Emissions

1 kW PV system will offset 16 kg of NO_2, 9 kg of SO_2, and 2300 kg of CO_2.

When power goes out, I still get power

When the power goes out, you will not get power. This is a safety issue with the repair man from the utility service. He does not like to work with live wires!

Won't work in the winter

PV systems work more efficiently in the winter than in the summer. Thermal systems will get you at least 50% of your requirement.

Solar can do everything right now

I am sorry to say that a PV system will not run my car. The day is coming.

Solar systems need batteries to store energy

If you have an off-grid system, you will need batteries. If you are on the grid, batteries are not required, or even used. The utility is your backup.

Rocket science installations

Solar energy systems are being sold in pre-engineered, packaged systems with everything you're going to need, including an instruction manual to make your installation actually easy.

Solar only works because of the government assistance

I must agree, that without rebates the industry would be a lot smaller, so I would like to say thank you to the United States government for assisting the country in getting Solar energy to the masses.

Solar is useless at night

PV systems have net metering. Solar thermal systems have storage tanks. If you are off-grid, batteries will be your source of fuel for the night.

The Solar Advocate

Federal government - 30% tax credit on PV systems-no limit.
Federal government - 30% tax credit on thermal systems-no limit.
State government-call to inquire.
Local utility-call to inquire.
The website for a complete list by state is http://www.dsireusa.org

Did You Know
Below 16,000 feet, the Earth is too hot for oil to exist? This is not a problem for natural gas.

Really!
Use of Solar energy will reduce health costs by reducing all the pollutants we are putting in the air, and potentially preventing people from getting sick.

Energy Facts
At the rate the United States is using PV, by 2020, Solar should be a $15 billion industry with over 150,000 new high-paying jobs.

Do the Math

Appliance	kWh/yr	Cost
Refrigerator – old	1800	$360
Refrigerator – new	550	$110-$260 savings/yr
AC – old	2200	$440
AC – new	1400	$280-$160 savings/yr
Dryer – old	1200	$240
Dryer – new	125	$25-$218 savings/yr

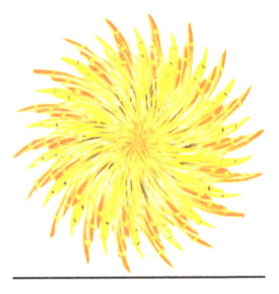

Solar Future

Solarized Cars

An "Enviormentally Green" Leader - Thanks President Obama

PV Fabric

Flying ?

Modern Outdoor Lighting

Solar Ideas I Am Keeping My Eyes On

- **Nano "Paint" Technology** – I am waiting for the day that my electric demand is being generated by the "paint" I applied to the east, south, and west sides of my home or business.
- **PV Shingles** are available today, with huge potential for higher PV efficiencies, and lower costs.
- **Higher PV Efficiency** – PVs efficiency is improving every year with the advancement of manufacturing process.
- **Multi-Level PV Cells** – PVs will be able to use more than the visible light of the Solar spectrum to generate electricity. This technology has been advanced by the PV cells designed for the Mars Rover! Thanks NASA!
- **Thin Film PV** – Will get more efficient, and I'm sure the price will continue to go down.
- **Building Integrated Photovoltaics (BIPV)** – Will become less custom, and more "off the shelf," which will reduce initial costs.
- **PV Awning Systems** – Let's generate electricity from the Sun I am blocking from getting into my home.

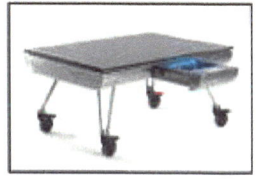

I hope it doesn't come to this!

Modules to Tables?

64   Odor Free   64

After the numerous years I have been working with Solar energy, I have never questioned a system smelling. I have never received a complaint that a Solar system smelled. Like I have said in the past, Solar systems do not have chimneys.

Did You Know

Solar energy does not contribute to smog, global warming, or acid rain?

Really!

Solar domestic hot water systems can save approximately 11.7 barrels of oil per year. That amount equates to a car driving 12,000 miles per year.

Energy Facts

1 ft^3 of natural gas equals 1000 BTU.
5600 ft^3 of natural gas equals one barrel of oil (42 gallons).

WOW

Thermal collectors and PV modules are available in various colors for improved aesthetics.

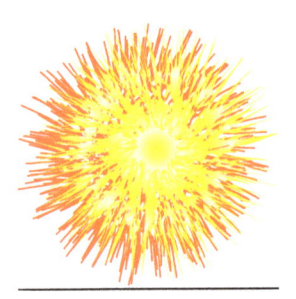  

Solar Disadvantages/No-No's

People claim that there are disadvantages to Solar energy. These have been some concerns from the field. :

- **Night** We cannot generate energy from the Sun at night, but we can surely store it. On the thermal side, most systems have storage tanks included, and on the PV side, you can always install batteries.
- **High Initial Costs** Solar energy systems have high INITIAL costs. Within a year's time, the federal government is giving a 30% discount in tax credits for qualified buyers. The states are also offering tax credits and rebates to help with these costs. Depending on where you live, you will receive a bare minimum of 30%, with some states raising that to 50-60%.
- **Local Building Codes** There is a town very close to where I live that will not permit any type of equipment on the front roof. That's including Solar! I believe the current green environment will change these laws, hopefully sooner than later.
- **Special Interest Groups** Oil, gas, coal, and nuclear to name a few. The Solar lobby is getting stronger every day. We got the Energy Bill passed!

Solar No-No's:

- **Installing Solar Equipment Facing North** Don't!
- **Roof Loads** Always confirm with installer that the roof and attic will be able to hold the extra weight of the equipment that you will be installing. If you are installing a thermosyphon system, remember a 50 gallon storage tank in your attic could possibly weigh as much as 450 pounds! Communicate with your installer on this issue.
- **Leaking Pipes** Make sure your plumber is licensed, insured, and experienced. There is no reason for leaky pipes!
- **Improper Wiring** Make sure your electrician is licensed, insured, and experienced. There is no reason for improper wiring!
- **Equipment Should Be Free of Shade** Solar collectors and modules hate shade. An example of what not to do:

DON'T INSTALL COLLECTORS IN FRONT OF A TREE!!

These concentrating collectors have been facing west for the past 8

- **Pool Cover Before Solar Pool System** Even though I sell Solar equipment, a good pool cover should always be used before a Solar pool system is installed. The combination of both is the real deal.
- **Don't Buy the Lowest Bid** I have found in my experience that "you get what you pay for." A good system will last at least 30+ years. I'm pretty sure that your low bidder will not guarantee these results.
- **Is System Working Properly?** If not, get it fixed!

65	Sustainable	65

Solar energy is sustainable because it will be able to replenish itself every day. Solar will be able to meet its current needs and have enough energy for generations to come.

Did You Know

Cars emit 1 pound of CO_2 into the atmosphere for each mile driven?

Really!

Life on Earth would not exist without the Sun.

Energy Facts

In San Antonio, Texas, a 10 kW PV system will save:
15.3 pounds of NO_2
37.9 pounds of SO_2
10.2 tons of CO_2
4, 300 gallons of water

WOW

The luminosity of the Sun is approximately 4×10^{33} erg/s. That is as bright as 4 trillion trillion 100 Watt light bulbs.

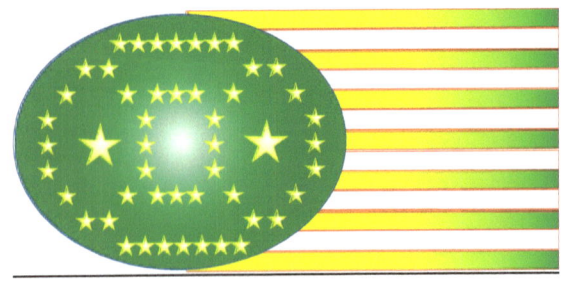

Conversions

1kW = 1000 Watts = 1.0×10^3 K. W = **1 kilowatt**
1MW = 1,000,000 Watts = 1.0×10^6 W = **1 megawatt**
1GW = 1,000,000,000 Watts = 1.0×10^9 W = **1 gigawatt**
1TW = 1,000,000,000,000 Watts = 1.0×10^{12} W = **1 terawatt**

Energy Conversions			
	BTU	kWh	therm
BTU	1	0.00029	0.00001
kWh	3412	1	29.308
therm	100,000	29.308	1
MBTU	1,000,000	293.08	10

Length & Distances Conversions					
	ft	in	m	mi	yd
ft	1	12	0.3048	0.00018939	0.333
in	0.083	1	0.0254	1.5×10^{-5}	0.027
m	3.28	39.37	1	6.213×10^{-4}	1.09
mi	5280	63360	1609.3	1	1760
yd	3	36	0.914	5.6×10^{-4}	1

Area Conversion			
	ft^2	in^2	m^2
ft²	1	144	0.092
in²	0.0069	1	6.45×10^{-4}
m²	10.76	1550	1

Volume Conversions					
	ft^3	gal	in^3	L	m^3
ft^3	1	7.48	1728	28.31	0.0283
gal	0.133	1	231	3.785	0.00378
in^3	5.7×10^{-4}	0.0043	1	0.016	1.6×10^{-5}
L	0.035	0.264	61.02	1	0.001
m^3	35.31	264.17	61023	1000	1

The Solar Advocate

The higher the energy prices, the more affordable Solar energy will be. When a barrel of oil hit $140 per barrel last year, I thought we were permanently in the affordable situation. Welcome to the politics of oil, which affects my pocketbook.

Did You Know
Solar energy domestic hot water systems will operate just about everywhere in the United States?

Really!
1 billionth of the Sun's Energy strikes the Earth.

Energy Facts
Hydropower is competitive with fossil fuel.

Really!
Due to improved research and development, and increases in sales, PV have declined in price every year.

Formulas and Additional Facts

Formulas for Area

Area of a Parallelogram = bh
Area of a circle = πr^2
Area of an ellipse = $\pi \times r1 \times r2$
Area of a triangle = ½ bh
Area of trapezoid = h/2 (b1+b2)

Formulas for Volume

Volume of a cube = a^3
Volume of a rectangle = abc
Volume of a cylinder = $\pi r^2 h$
Volume of a sphere = $4/3\pi r^3$

Formulas for Surface Area

Surface area for a cube = $6A^2$
Surface Area Of a Rectangle = 2ab + 2bc + 2ac
Surface area of a sphere = $4\pi r^2$
Surface area of a cylinder = $2\pi r^2 + 2\pi rh$

Additional Facts used in book

1 Horse Power = 750 Watts

1 Barrel of Oil = 42 Gallons

7.33 Barrels of Oil = 1 metric Ton

The average weight of coal in one train car = 50,000 pounds

Speed of Sound = 768 mph

Speed of Light = 186,000 mi/s

Population of the United States as of August 23, 2009 = 307,253,577
      This is an increase of 684,512 people since May 1, 2009!!!!!!

Population of the world as of August 23, 2009 = 6,779,526,662

Area of the United States = 3,717,727 mi^2

Total number of automobiles in the United States = 247,254,605

The End

The Solar Advocate

INDEX (Subjects)

INDEX

Characteristics of Solar Energy